Books by Arlene Hale

WHERE THE HEART IS

WHERE THE HEART IS

༄ઌૢૡ

by Arlene Hale

LITTLE, BROWN AND COMPANY — BOSTON — TORONTO

FIRST EDITION

T 02/74

Library of Congress Cataloging in Publication Data

Hale, Arlene.
  Where the heart is.

  I. Title.
PZ4.H1618Wi ₍PS3515.A262₎   813'.5'4   73-16100
ISBN 0-316-33876-1

Published simultaneously in Canada
by Little, Brown & Company (Canada) Limited

PRINTED IN THE UNITED STATES OF AMERICA

For Betty
and
all those days of yore

Home's not merely four square walls,
    Though with pictures hung and gilded;
Home is where Affection calls —
    Filled with shrines the Heart hath builded.

— CHARLES SWAIN

WHERE THE HEART IS

1

SONDRA TRACY had been in Tokyo for two days and had spent nearly every waking moment in the business of buying merchandise for Imports, Inc. Her boss in Los Angeles, Harry Chapman, would be pleased with her progress. It was the middle of the afternoon when she returned to her hotel to take stock of her various transactions. Later in the evening she would have dinner with Mr. Moji. If she sealed the arrangement she wanted with him, she would feel she'd done very well. From Tokyo, she would go to Rome and London.

Reaching her hotel, Sondra was stopped by the man behind the front desk.

"Miss Tracy," he said in his very correct English. "We have a cable for you."

It would be from Harry. He'd already cabled her twice for additional merchandise he wanted her to try and obtain. Usually, his wires meant just that many more headaches and that many more contacts for her to make. Negotiations weren't always that easy, a fact Harry blithely ignored.

Still, Sondra loved her work. She liked to think that in

the two years she had worked for Harry, she had added something special to Imports, Inc. Harry had always done the buying in the past, but the last three times he had trusted her to handle it, and in Harry's book this was the same as high praise.

"So, I'm getting bored with overseas travel," Harry shrugged. "You like it, so you do it, Sondra."

Before going to Los Angeles, Sondra had worked for an interior decorator in her hometown, Lewiston, in the Midwest. She'd gone to Los Angeles intending to continue in that line of work. But when she'd been unable to find anything satisfactory, she'd answered Harry's newspaper ad. The minute she'd walked into his shop, she'd fallen in love with the place, cluttered as it was, crammed with every kind of collector's object she could think of, just waiting for someone to love and appreciate it and bring some order to it.

"Or was it that I was just desperate?" she sometimes asked herself.

Harry's shop had quickly become more than just an interesting place to work. It had become her haven, her hiding place, her second home.

Now here she was in Tokyo and it was unbelievable.

"What *am* I doing here?" she wondered with a sigh. "Sondra Tracy in Tokyo! It's mad."

When she reached her hotel room and unlocked the door, she fought away the urge to simply drop across the bed and sleep. The time change had her weary to the bone and her days and nights were all mixed up. But first things first.

She called for a pot of hot, scented tea, and then got down to work, spreading her papers on the tiny lacquered

desk. But she couldn't concentrate. What strange things happened in a person's life! She'd had her roots so solidly in Lewiston and the house on Wyler Street where she had lived most of her life. She had always been one of those ridiculously imbedded homebodies with no desire to spread her wings and fly away. But spread them she had, and fly away she did.

"Don't go," Gretta had said. "You'll regret it someday. Stay here and face the music, work it out. Run away now and you'll never stop running."

"I can't stay," she remembered saying. "I *can't!*"

She told herself she wouldn't think about Lewiston. But it was impossible to crush down the quick mental images that sprang up into her mind, like mushrooms after a warm, spring rain.

Lewiston was lovely in its own way. She always thought of the wide, rippling Mississippi River dotted with sandy islands, carrying lengthy barges downward to the Gulf. After they passed the waterfront, they slid past the high cliffs of DeReuss Park, a cool, tree-lined place where fountains and statues stood in quiet dignity.

Lewiston was fresh Sunday mornings with sunlight on the church spires, tennis courts, the campus, the lake, the flat, fertile surrounding countryside. But some of her fondest memories were walking up Wyler Street just two short blocks to Carrie Winterhall's house. A tender smile touched Sondra's face. Carrie had been like a great aunt, or a godmother. She was always the same, a treasure, a joy. Oh, the lovely, lovely hours she had spent there!

"You make my day, Sondra," Carrie had always told her. "I sit by the window and watch for you coming up the street."

Carrie was the bright side of the story. Other memories were like plunging into a deep, cold sea where she had to swim for her life.

For Lewiston was also Cleve Ridgeway. She could not and would not think of him or the unhappy, unforgivable past. It was Mother and Dad and a dark, angry, wounded time in her life.

She forced her thoughts away from the past and back to the present, to the swanky Japanese hotel room and the work on her desk. She remembered the cable and ripped it open to see what Harry wanted this time. With instant shock, she saw that it was not from Harry at all, but from Quentin Hancock, an attorney at home.

"What on earth —"

She scanned the message quickly, drawing a sharp breath, brushing back a lock of blond hair in a dazed fashion.

"Carrie Winterhall passed away. Service two o'clock Wednesday. Request your presence for reading of will immediately following."

Sondra crumpled the cable. It couldn't be true. This couldn't have happened! Then she smoothed the cable again and reread it. Instant grief touched her, making her eyes brim with tears and the room spin. Not Carrie! Oh, she couldn't lose Carrie too!

For several shocked moments Sondra couldn't move. She sat at the desk, staring out the window, but seeing nothing. She knew she had to make plans. If she was to get there in time, there was no place for tears now. She made her plane reservation, sent an answering cable to Quentin Hancock and then put in an overseas call to Harry.

It took some time. At last she heard Harry's sleepy, grumpy voice on the other end of the line.

"Hello, Harry. It's Sondra."

"Why are you calling me at this ungodly hour? Do you know what time it is?"

"It's afternoon in Tokyo."

"And it's the middle of the night here! What is it?"

She explained.

"I see," Harry said. "Hancock phoned here for you. I told him how to reach you. But that was yesterday morning."

"I just now got the cable. There must have been some crazy delay. Harry, I'm flying to Chicago within a couple of hours. I'm not sure when I can get back to L.A. If you want to pick up the rest of the buying —"

"No. Is it necessary you go?"

"Carrie was like family, Harry."

"All right. We'll talk about the buying when you get back. Keep in touch and don't be too long — okay?"

She made a few necessary local calls, hurriedly packed and made her plane with a few minutes to spare.

She did all of this in a stunned, numb sort of way. She folded the cable and thrust it in her purse, hiding it out of sight, as if being unable to see it would mean that the terrible news wasn't true.

Airborne, her thoughts were filled with Carrie. She didn't remember Carrie's husband, Kermit. He had been dead for many years. Carrie's only son, Phillip, was gone too, having died as a young man. Carrie had no immediate family left. Her life in these last years had not been happy, not since her husband and son had quarreled bitterly and Phillip had left Lewiston never to return.

Sondra wondered why it was that Quentin Hancock had asked her to be present for the reading of the will. Had Carrie left her a legacy? She smiled sadly. Perhaps the china closet and all those fragile cups hanging inside.

"Get your cup, Sondra. Any one you want," Carrie used to tell her. "And we'll have tea."

Even now she could remember the sweet turmoil of choosing the cup and she could smell the lemon slice, the pungent tea, feel the fragile china between her lips, holding the cup carefully for fear she would spill or worse yet, horror of horrors, drop the cup and break it.

But she had loved those afternoons as a little girl in Carrie's old-fashioned living room with the sun slanting through the huge maple trees in the front yard, dotting the Persian carpet, caressing Carrie's silky white hair, bouncing off crystal chandeliers and burnishing the polished oak floors.

From little girl to awkward junior, to gushing teenager, to a college coed achingly in love — all of those people who had once been Sondra Tracy had at one time or another found their way to Carrie's house and, once there, had spilled out all sorts of childish dreams, girlish hopes, womanly despairs.

Three hours out of Tokyo, they ran into bad weather and the pilot announced they would be taking another route north. It meant arriving behind schedule. Sondra sat with her hands tightly clasped, watching the time anxiously.

One delay came on the heels of another. When she finally reached Chicago, it was one-thirty and she had missed her connection to Lewiston. It meant she would not be home in time to pay her last respects to Carrie; this was one more pain to add to her grief.

She caught the next flight two hours later. She watched the familiar landscape from her window and found that the nearer she got to Lewiston, the harder her heart thundered. She had not been home since Dad died, more than a year ago. Mother was still in New Jersey. Her occasional letters kept them in touch but not much else. Coming home to Lewiston tore at Sondra's heart. What was here for her now? Now, even Carrie was gone. Link by link, the chain binding her to her hometown was being broken.

She would not think about Cleve. She dare not.

When the plane put down at the airport at last, she was surprised to see Quentin Hancock waiting for her. She walked swiftly toward him. He stretched out a hand.

"Hello, Miss Tracy," he said.

"I'm sorry I'm so late. I got here as quickly as I could."

"Yes. I know. You must be tired but would you mind coming to my office now?"

"Is the matter so urgent?"

"Not really, but I must be out of town for the next few days and if I could, I'd like to take care of this before I go."

Perhaps it was just as well. She was anxious to have this sad business over and done.

Quentin took her baggage to his car and helped her inside. They drove from the airport along the wide, sunny streets of Lewiston, each one achingly familiar, and downtown to his office.

There, sitting in a leather chair, gripping the arms with cold hands, she heard Carrie's last words.

"Having no other kith or kin, I bequeath to Sondra Tracy all of my holdings, properties and belongings to do with as she pleases. The pleasant hours she gave me so

unselfishly have never been forgotten, but treasured and cherished more than she can ever know. My blessings go with them."

Sondra lifted a startled face to Quentin Hancock.

"You mean, everything she had is now mine?"

"The entire estate," Quentin nodded. "The house on Wyler Street, the cottage on Reynolds Lake, a few investment holdings, considerable cash . . ."

"I can't believe it! I had no idea —"

"Carrie seemed secretly pleased about the whole affair the day I drew up this new will two years ago."

"About the time I left Lewiston!" Sondra murmured. "And before this current will . . ."

"In essence, she had left everything to charity and a few pet projects like the local college. There were some token sums for friends, you included."

"Then she changed it and gave it *all* to me! But why?"

"There was no one else she truly cared about. She told me that and of course there is no immediate family."

Sondra shook her blond head with a sigh. "I can't believe it!"

"Carrie had her will and her way," Quentin smiled.

Sondra rubbed her fingers across her eyes. "But Carrie had a son —"

"Phillip Winterhall has been dead for several years."

"I know," Sondra said. "He married a woman Carrie didn't approve of. But what I'm getting at is, I think there was a grandson."

Quentin Hancock frowned. "I've heard nothing about a grandson."

"But I remember talk in the neighborhood — there were rumors — not that Carrie ever told me herself, but I think there *was* a child born to Phillip Winterhall."

Quentin shook his head. "It wouldn't matter if that were true, Miss Tracy. Carrie's will is legal and binding. You are her only heir."

Sondra gripped her hands together, trying to stop their trembling. "But I *know* how Carrie loved Phillip and she would never turn away from her own flesh and blood!"

"I think you've just answered your own questions, Miss Tracy," Quentin said. "If there had been a grandson, she would have remembered him in the will. More than likely the rumors were false to begin with."

"But there is a remote possibility, isn't there, that a grandson exists?"

"I doubt it."

"I want the story checked, Mr. Hancock," Sondra said. "Thoroughly. I want to know."

"Why would you want to do that? You don't seem to understand that Carrie has made you a women of means! It's not an exorbitant legacy perhaps, but still a sizable one."

Sondra shook her head. She was unable to focus, to concentrate. It had all come too fast. Now this last development was more than she could comprehend.

"Please, could we wait for another day?" she asked.

Mr. Hancock nodded. "Of course. I shouldn't have rushed you with this. My fault. I'm sorry. But I thought you would want to know. We'll wait a few days and when I'm back in the city, we'll talk again. In the meanwhile, accept it or not, everything Carrie owned is now yours. I've closed and locked the house on Wyler Street. I'll give you the keys to it and to the Wild Willow cottage on the lake."

He took the keys from his desk drawer and gave them to her. She held them tightly in her cold, closed fist.

Somehow in that moment, she knew truly and forever that Carrie was gone, that this wasn't happening in some kind of bad dream.

"I took the liberty of arranging for a room at the Hotel Lewiston. I'll drive you there, if you like."

She wanted to cry out in fresh protest. Not the Hotel Lewiston! But she was too tired to argue, to ask him to get her a room elsewhere. She could go to Gretta's, but somehow, before seeing her oldest and dearest friend, she needed to be alone, to gather her strength. Right now, she simple wanted to go into some quiet room, close the door and lock away the world before she collapsed.

"Besides, there's no reason why I should expect to see Cleve at the hotel," she told herself. "Just because he lives there. I'll be in and out before he even knows I'm in town."

Quentin drove her to the hotel and saw her inside. There, he shook her hand.

"I'll be in touch within the next few days, Miss Tracy."

"Thank you. For everything."

She signed the register and realized it was dinner time. She wanted something to eat, then long, long hours of sleep. Perhaps then she could come to terms with everything that had happened. She tipped the bellboy to take her luggage to her room and went into the Coffee Shop.

A few curious customers spied her. Some nodded, recognizing her. But there were no close friends, no one that required more than a polite hello.

"Thank God for that!" she thought tiredly. "I'm not up to small talk tonight."

The coffee was hot and strong. She drank two cups of it before she tried eating the food on her plate. She was hungry from her long and anxious trip home, but she

couldn't eat. She couldn't seem to get the food past her lips. She gave it up and asked the waitress for more coffee.

Then, as if the nightmare hadn't already been nerve-jangling enough, she sensed that Cleve was near. She looked up and found him standing in the doorway.

He scanned the room with his gray eyes. He wore a light suit perfectly tailored and a tie that was blue. His hair was black, thick, brushed neatly, falling on his fore-head with a soft wave.

There was strength about him and a hard set to his shoulders that was proof he intended to push his way through the world with no nonsense. As he made his way to a table, he nodded to a few acquaintances, stopped to say hello and chat for a few moments.

She wondered if she could escape without being seen. Then he turned his head sharply, quickly, and his gray eyes flashed with recognition. He straightened. His shoulders became firmer, his chin harder. For a moment, she thought he would ignore her. She hoped and prayed that he would.

Then she saw that he had no such intention. He started toward her. She wanted the floor to open up and devour her, to spare her these next few minutes.

He paused at her table, a quiet shadow. Then he put his palms on the tabletop and leaned toward her, his eyes commanding her gaze and holding it.

"So, you've come home," he said.

She lifted her chin. "Just passing through."

"Because we've lost Carrie?"

She nodded. "Yes."

His face softened and she saw despair in his eyes.

"I'm sorry, really sorry. I'm going to miss her."

"So am I."

The moment hung heavily between them and yesterday was a heartbeat away.

He seemed about to say more. But then he straightened, gave her another quick glance, a nod, and moved away. She saw him take a table and begin to study the menu with undivided attention.

She put her head back for a moment, eyes closed, wrung out. Then, as quickly as she could, she gathered her things and rushed away. She managed to hold back the tears until she reached her room.

2

PERHAPS IT WAS just as well that the encounter was over. If at all possible, she would not see Cleve again. The last time they met had been at Dad's funeral. There had been compassion on his face when he came to speak to her, to hold her hand for a moment in his.

"If there's anything I can do, Sondra, please tell me."

"No. What is there to do now?" she had asked.

"I wish I could help somehow, someway."

His voice had touched some deep need inside her. For those few minutes it was as if nothing had happened between them. If he hadn't moved away when he had, she might have flung herself into his arms. Now, just a few minutes ago, when he spoke of Carrie she felt the same need, the same desire. But it was all over between them. There was only anger and bitterness left. But her emotions could trick her and make her do foolish things. She would have to be on guard while she was here. She thought of Gretta and changed her mind about waiting until the next day to get in touch with her. She needed the sound of her friend's voice.

She reached for the phone, put in the call and got Gretta's answering service.

"I'd like to speak with Dr. Berglund. Is there any chance of that? I'm an old friend from out of town."

"I'm sorry, Dr. Berglund is on an emergency call at the hospital. It's difficult to say how long she'll be. Would you like to leave a message?"

"No. I think not. Thank you. I'll get in touch with her tomorrow."

Everything waited for tomorrow. Tomorrow she would see Gretta and tomorrow she would have to go to Carrie's house.

Sondra went to stand under a warm shower, trying to relax, feeling the tiredness of her desperate flight creeping into her bones. The unnerving meeting with Cleve had been a final blow.

She did not sleep well despite her fatigue. Several times she awakened, not certain where she was, then remembering all too quickly what had brought her here. Each time she awakened and remembered her legacy, she asked herself why. Why had Carrie left it all to her?

The next morning, rather than risk seeing Cleve again, she ordered breakfast in her room. Then she slipped out of the hotel and walked a block to a car rental agency. There she picked out a convertible and quickly drove away.

She noticed several streets were barricaded. Some kind of construction work was being done. She found her way to Valor Street, anxious to see Gretta. Knowing her old friend as she did, she knew Gretta would be at the office early.

Dr. Gretta Berglund! The name made Sondra smile with pride.

"It's going to be an uphill battle all the way, Sondra," Gretta used to say, her small chin lifted with determination. "But I'm going to get there!"

And now she had. She had overcome all the obstacles in her path. Although Gretta was older, they had been friends most of their lives. They had grown up in the same neighborhood and Gretta had been the older sister that Sondra had never had.

Gretta had opened an office in Lewiston more than a year ago, and as Sondra parked her car and walked up to the fashionable professional building, she found herself filled with anticipation.

The waiting room was empty. The door marked Private was closed but Sondra knocked lightly.

"Gretta, are you in there? It's me, Sondra."

She wasn't surprised when she heard Gretta's quick steps. The door came open. Gretta was small, a plain woman with fine, blue-gray, compassionate eyes and a smile that could warm the hearts of young and old alike.

"Sondra!" Gretta said.

Sondra found herself clinging to the smaller woman for a moment and when they drew away from each other, there were tears in their eyes.

"What a terrible thing to bring you home," Gretta said. "I didn't get to the services yesterday. A baby decided to be born at that precise time."

"My plane was delayed. I didn't get there either, Gretta."

"Oh, no!"

"I still can't believe it's happened. I can't imagine the house on Wyler Street without Carrie —"

"Nor can I," Gretta said gently. "Come in and sit down. Close the door. You look tired, Sondra."

"It was a long flight home from Tokyo."

"Tokyo?"

Sondra nodded and explained how Quentin Hancock's cable had brought her home.

"Have you heard the rest of it?" Sondra asked. "Carrie left me her entire estate."

Gretta stared at her for a moment.

"Aren't you surprised?" Sondra asked.

"I suppose I should be and yet, when you think about it, it's a logical thing for her to have done. Carrie adored you, even as a little girl. You two had something very special. I'm glad for you, Sondra."

"I was never so stunned in my life!"

"It was what Carrie wanted or it wouldn't have been left that way."

"I must go to the house today and I'm dreading it. It will seem so empty without her —" Sondra's voice broke and for a moment she struggled to compose herself. Gretta put a cool hand over hers.

"Would you like me to come with you? Perhaps I could find some spare time —"

Sondra shook her head. "No. Thank you. I think I have to do this alone."

That was the way it was these days, she went alone — and had ever since she left Lewiston two years ago, an unhappy, unstable young woman who found it difficult to trust her emotions and just as difficult to warm up to anyone new in any special way. She had dated several men in L.A. and she had made new friends. But she had no friend like Gretta, and no man had become as important to her as Cleve had been in Lewiston.

"Tell me, are you really happy in Los Angeles?" Gretta asked.

"I have a good job and a nice boss. He gives me more responsibility every day. Now, I do the traveling to Japan, Rome, London —"

"But working in an import shop was never what you wanted to do. Your line of talents ran to interior decorating."

"But the imports are fun too, Gretta."

"Why don't you come home?" Gretta asked gently. "You belong here. You always have and you always will."

Sondra shook her head. "I can't."

"Because of Cleve?"

"Because of many things. As luck would have it, I saw him at the hotel last night."

"He's well thought of at the college and he's managed to bring in private donations and endowments in the thousands of dollars."

"Cleve was always persuasive." Sondra said with a wry smile.

"The way I hear it, Ed DeReuss wants him to work for him."

"Is he interested?"

"I don't really know. But knowing Ed DeReuss, Cleve is probably having the pressure put on him. Then, too, there's Valerie —"

Sondra met Gretta's direct gaze.

"You're trying to tell me something."

"Cleve and Valerie are seeing a great deal of each other these days."

"Oh."

"You shouldn't have let what happened come between you and Cleve, Sondra."

Sondra clenched her hands together.

"What's past is past, Gretta. Let's leave it there."

Gretta gave her a long look. "Yes. You're right. I shouldn't have mentioned it. You've already got enough on your mind."

"Tell me about you," Sondra said. "It looks very successful around here, this nice office — and you so professional in that coat —"

"More patients every day," Gretta said, pleased. "I'm building a good practice. I'm very grateful for the way people have taken to me. I love every minute of my work."

Sondra looked at her watch. She knew that soon Gretta would be busy with her appointments. It was time to go, whether she wanted to or not.

"I'm off," she said. "I'll phone."

"Don't let it upset you too much at Carrie's house, Sondra. And I'd better warn you. You'll find the old neighborhood changed. They're building a new freeway through the heart of Lewiston."

"Can't they leave well enough alone?"

Gretta laughed. "Progress will not be stopped. Some in town aren't happy with the idea, others are all for it. So, there you are —"

Sondra waved good-bye to Gretta and stepped out into the morning, bright with sunlight. She paused for a moment. From here she couldn't see the river but she was conscious of it all the same. Waking at the hotel that morning, the first thing she had done was to go to her window and peer out to its gray waters, watching it rippling along, the bridge across it rumbling with early traffic, a speedboat cutting a wake as it roared downstream.

The air was humid. This was something else she had

forgotten, but there was no smog here and the air smelled fresh and clean.

She drove in the direction of Wyler Street and again saw that several of the streets were blocked off. A new freeway!

"Why can't they leave well enough alone?" Sondra wondered again with a frown.

On impulse, when she reached Wyler Street, she turned south instead of north toward Carrie's house. She wanted to see the house where she had lived, where she had grown up. Although the house had been sold after Dad died, and someone else had moved in, in her own mind the house was hers, it was home.

She felt keen anticipation as she drove down the street. Then, suddenly, she came to a barricade and had to put on the brakes.

"What's this!" she said. "Is this as far as I can go?" With a cry of alarm, she got out of the car, moved the barricade and stepped through. Just beyond she could see a large gaping hole that stretched out so far it had surely eaten up two blocks or more in width.

She spun about. Where once their house had stood there was nothing!

"Oh, no!" she gasped. "No!"

She stared, not quite trusting her eyes. But there were no trees, no flowers, no sidewalk, no house or front porch, nothing but rubble and the broken walls of what had once been their basement.

Her ears were singing. Why hadn't Gretta warned her?

She could hear the sound of bulldozers working down in the gaping hole, hollowing out more earth. She heard the rumble of cement trucks and saw a crew of men work-

ing. Still, she could not believe the house was gone. Here she had grown into a young woman. Here Dad had rocked her on his knee and told her stories. Here Gretta had been a very frequent visitor, regarding the place as her own home. Here Cleve had come to steal away her heart and her love!

Beneath her feet, she felt the earth tremble. With a start, she cast a glance over her shoulder. The machine looked monstrously huge and it was bearing down on her. With a shout of alarm, she jumped out of the way. The driver saw her. Angrily, he stopped the machine and leaped down and walked toward her.

"Lady! This is a restricted area! What are you doing here? Didn't you see the barricades?" he shouted above the noise of the machine.

He was a tall, big-shouldered man with a rugged, sun-tanned face and angry brown eyes. He wore tan work clothes and heavy boots. He wore a yellow hard hat that had R. WAGNER stenciled across it in black paint.

"I could have killed you, do you know that?"

"Did you do this?" she asked, waving at the pile of rubble that had once been her home.

"I did and I've got to finish it," he said with a curt nod. "Now, if you don't want to get run over, lady, I suggest you go!"

"I have every right to be here," she shouted back angrily. "I *belong* here!"

"Not since nine months ago. All of this was bought and paid for then. Now, if you've got some legal complaint, you're barking up the wrong tree. Who are you, the former owner?"

"This was my *home!*" she said, knowing she sounded childishly ridiculous and tearful.

"Sorry. I've got to get busy, Miss. I'm running behind schedule and the front office is yelling its head off. Now, if you don't mind — clear out!"

She turned away. In a moment, she heard the bulldozer roar into action again and the grinding, crunching sound of concrete being flattened and reduced to rubble.

She hated R. Wagner with a hate that shook her to the depths of her soul. She hated the freeway. She felt physically ill. Everything was changing before her eyes. There was a nameless terror welling up in her throat, stifling her, chilling her. If home wasn't here, where was it? The house was gone. Home was gone. Where did she belong?

3

SONDRA MADE herself climb into the convertible without another look at the cloud of dust that rose up from the spot where their house had once stood. For a moment, she clenched the steering wheel with cold hands, needing the feel of something solid. She felt immobile, flattened, squeezed so hard she couldn't breathe.

Somehow she got the car started and turned around. She drove north. When she reached Carrie's house, she turned in at the driveway and shut off the motor. It was like some horrible nightmare that wouldn't end. Now she must go inside the house, and she knew this too was going to be painful.

Slowly, she made herself look around. Everything was so dearly familiar and, thank God, it looked the same. Nothing had changed here. The sight of the old-fashioned veranda across the front of the house and the tall door with the fancy glass window seemed to calm her. So many times in the past she had come here, heavy of heart, and Carrie had managed to make her smile and see the brighter side of things.

"Help me now, Carrie," Sondra whispered to herself.

The key went smoothly in the lock. With a click the door came open. She paused and looked down the shadowy, cool hallway. The house had its own fragrances of old lavender, a scent Carrie had used, the lemon from the polish rubbed into the furniture. Then there was an unidentifiable spice found in the tea Carrie always served, a tinge of cinnammon, a flashing of jasmine.

But it was so empty, so quiet. The kettle should have been singing in the kitchen, ready for tea. Carrie's rocker should have been making little squeaking noises, or her voice should be heard as she talked on the phone or called from some other part of the house.

Gripping the key in her hand, Sondra moved deeper into the house. She paused beside Carrie's favorite chair. A piece of needlepoint waited on the table where she had placed it. Sondra touched it with trembling fingers.

"Carrie's house is like another world," Cleve used to tell her. "As if in many ways, time had stopped for her."

Yet, Carrie had been a modern, lively, bright-eyed woman who knew what was going on. True, part of her clung to past, happier years, when her son Phillip had still lived here. But Carrie had never grieved over those years openly. She had lifted her chin and met everyone with a direct look and a ready smile. For Sondra her arms had been open and waiting, and she had walked into them, needing the special love that had grown between them.

Quietly, solemnly, Sondra went into each room. Then, when she reached the kitchen, which somehow was the most symbolic of Carrie, she found it flooded with the morning sunlight. It was so cheerful and pleasant that the cloud began to lift. Sondra took a deep breath. The last thing Carrie would have wanted was for her to feel sad.

"Each day is a present from God," Carrie used to say.

"Oh, why do so many spend them so foolishly, so recklessly? Don't they know what a treasure they are?"

Sondra blinked back the tears and was thankful that her good sense made her see things here as they really were. For one, the house was a gold mine of antiques. Her experience in Imports, Inc., kept telling her that. Each piece was old, valuable and in perfect condition.

What would she do with all of this? She found herself reaching for the phone. When she called Gretta's office, she had to wait for a moment or two and then she heard Gretta's reassuring voice on the other end of the line.

"Forgive me for bothering you. I know you're busy."

"I rather expected to hear from you. Are you all right?"

"Yes. I suppose so. Gretta, I had forgotten there was so much furniture here, so many dishes and knickknacks and God knows what all. I'm overwhelmed. I don't know what to do first."

"There's a firm in town, Webb and Company. They have a very competent woman working for them. Maxine Davis. She's a patient of mine. She'll come and catalog and appraise everything if you want."

"That sounds like a good idea. Mr. Hancock told me we'd need a complete list of furnishings for tax purposes. Perhaps I'll give her a call."

"Why don't you? I think it might save you a lot of time and I know you'd like Maxine."

"Well, not today. I don't really think I want to face any of this just yet. I've about decided to go out to the lake and stay at Wild Willow while I'm here."

"That's also a very good idea," Gretta said. "Call me this evening, will you?"

They said good-bye and hung up. Sondra spent only a few minutes longer at the house, then relocked the door

and drove back downtown. She checked out of the hotel and was relieved not to see Cleve again.

Wild Willow was a snug cottage on Reynolds Lake where she had spent many a happy hour. Memories of Carrie were sure to be there too, but not like at the house on Wyler Street. Sondra enjoyed the short drive to the lake and was almost eager for the first glimpse of the blue water. It was a good place to relax, to gather her thoughts, to come to terms with the situation.

As she turned down the road that would follow the lakefront and lead to Wild Willow, she was startled to see that progress was taking its hold here too. The Grandview Hotel, situated on the water, drew hundreds of vacationers every summer. Now, right next door, there seemed to be a lot of activity. She saw that the earth had been scarred with bulldozers and pushed and shaped like a huge wad of bread dough until it had been formed roughly into a large golf course. From the look of things, there were to be tennis courts too and a sprawling clubhouse. As she drove by, she could hear electric saws and constant hammering.

Wild Willow was but a short half mile farther down the road. The cottage, when she reached it, was showing signs of neglect. It was naturally rustic in design and overlooked Reynolds Lake, but she realized that Carrie had let the place go. Only the grass and weeds had been kept down — a dozen other small things needed to be done.

"Carrie was no longer able to care for it," Sondra realized. "I didn't know she was so ill!"

She was apprehensive about going inside. But when she unlocked the back door and stepped in, she saw that it was tidy and neat. Apparently Carrie had kept Mrs. Fulton, the cleaning lady, in her employ.

"What's that?" Sondra asked herself.

Had she heard something in one of the other rooms? For a moment, fear gripped her. It was eerie enough coming here like this without hearing strange sounds. She took her courage in hand and went to the living room.

"Mrs. Fulton, is that you?"

There was no reply. Was the front door just closing? But when she went to try it, she found it locked. A quick glance through the glass in the door revealed no one. It must have been her imagination. Still, it gave her an unpleasant feeling.

Inside the cottage was unchanged. It seemed smaller than she remembered, but the stone fireplace was as lovely as ever. The fur rug lay in front and the comfortable couch squatted before the hearth just as it always had.

"I love you," Cleve had told her that day as they watched the fire blazing, the snow falling outside the window. "I love you more than I can tell you."

She remembered his lips, so warm and sweet against her own. They had been ice skating on the lake and then had gone inside Carrie's cottage, stamping their cold feet and rubbing their hands. Cleve built the fire while she made hot chocolate. Carrie kept the cottage open year around, mostly for Sondra's use.

"You're mine, you know," Cleve had said. "You'll never belong to anyone else."

"I wouldn't want to."

"Let's not wait. Let's get married now."

"No. Dad wouldn't permit it. Besides, you must finish college. You know that. It's hard enough without a wife —"

"That's a nice sound. My wife," he said.

They had stayed there until the fire burned low, the logs fell into embers and the night crept up with black skies and brilliant stars.

Of all the times they'd had together, somehow that day stayed in Sondra's mind as the most important of all.

She tore her thoughts away. Why remember it now? It was over and by her own doing. She had not known that day that she could be so vulnerable, so hurt by anything. She thought nothing could tear her away from Cleve. But, as so many times before, she had been wrong.

She walked into each room, realizing that she felt comfortable here, not uneasy as she had at Carrie's house. She would make this her headquarters until she could finish the business of Carrie's estate and go back to Los Angeles. She would have to tell Harry her plans and she didn't relish the idea.

The phone was always kept connected. She made the call to Los Angeles as brief as she could.

"How long will you be away?" Harry asked anxiously.

"I don't know. I'll come back as soon as I can. That's the best I can do now."

There must be some way she could speed things along. Perhaps Webb and Company was the right answer. She looked them up in the phone book and soon had Maxine Davis on the line. Mrs. Davis was pleasant and helpful. They made arrangements to meet at the house the next day at ten o'clock. It might be simplest to put the entire matter in her hands and go back to L.A. But could she bring herself to sell the furnishings, to dispose of the house? She truly didn't know.

Restless, she went outside. The sound of the construction work down the road reached her ears. She was curious. It felt good to stretch her legs, to follow the road

she knew so well, to hear the lapping of the water against the shore. A sailboat skimmed the horizon and a fisherman sat hunched in a flat-bottomed boat, intent on his line. Could that be a touch of autumn color in the very tops of the trees? So soon? Where had the summer gone?

As she reached the site of the new clubhouse, she paused to study it. It looked as if it was going to be very big and very fancy. A car pulled up alongside her.

"Sondra, is that you?"

Sondra took a long breath. She would know that voice anywhere. It could only belong to Valerie DeReuss.

Valerie climbed out of her car. She was flawlessly and expensively dressed, even though she wore casual sports clothes. Her dark hair was tied back by a bright band and her eyes were hidden behind huge, round sunglasses that dwarfed her beautiful face. She hadn't changed an iota, still tall, shapely and very much aware of who she was.

Sondra had known Valerie during her college days. She had arrived on the scene during Sondra's junior year. Before that, Valerie had gone east to school. The only reason she had decided to grace the local college with her shimmering presence was because the eastern college had kicked her out. Or so rumor had it. Strangely enough, they had been in the same general crowd at college, although they had never been good friends.

"How do you like my new baby?" Valerie asked, nodding toward the rising structure.

"Yours?" Sondra asked with surprise.

Valerie laughed and tossed her dark hair. "I was always nagging at Daddy to build something like this. We need some recreational facilities. Daddy finally said, all right, if you want it, you build it! So, here it is. A new golf course, new tennis courts. There will be game rooms and a

bowling alley inside the clubhouse. A sauna, a bar, maybe even a dining room later. A fun sort of place."

"I'm sure it's going to be impressive," Sondra said.

"Only the best will do," Valerie said with a smile. "I helped lay out the entire design. I come by every day to see how it's going. But I must say, I get annoyed sometimes. They're always behind schedule!"

"What is this, a new hobby, Valerie?"

Valerie gave her a quick look. "You might call it that. Then, too, I plan to have Daddy hire Cleve to manage it. That was really my motive from the beginning."

Valerie was watching Sondra very closely. Valerie knew, as did everyone in the old crowd, that she and Cleve had been serious about each other. But if Valerie expected to get a reaction from her now, she was badly mistaken. She wouldn't give Valerie the satisfaction.

"Cleve's being wasted at the college," Valerie said airily. "I'm sure he'll see the sense of that. Come along. I'll introduce you to the man I hired to put in charge of this little adventure. Lon Greene. See him over there? Don't you think he's handsome?"

Lon Greene was blond and sunburned. His shirt-sleeves were rolled to his elbows and his forearms were heavy and muscular. From beneath strong brows, his eyes were blue and quick.

"Lon, this is Sondra Tracy, an old college friend. She's from Los Angeles now. Sondra, Lon Greene."

A large hand came out to take hers in a quick, friendly handshake. She was aware of strength and warmth in his touch.

"Nice to know you, Sondra."

"I see you finished the west side," Valerie said. "Does that mean you're back on schedule?"

Lon Greene straightened and tucked a roll of blueprints more snugly under his arm. "No, but we're gaining."

Valerie frowned. "Really, Lon, I don't know what I'm going to do with you. Always behind schedule!"

Lon seemed unruffled. He gave Valerie a quick look. "We're doing our best. And when we've finished, you'll have something to be proud of."

A blaring car horn interrupted them. Valerie looked up and smiled.

"Ah, there's Cleve! I was afraid he'd be late. I want to show him the progress we've made," Valerie said.

Lon gave Valerie a polite smile. "I'm glad you think we've made *some* progress."

Valerie made a pretty face at him and waved to Cleve. Sondra braced herself for another painful meeting.

Cleve came striding toward them, tie flapping, his dark hair stirred by the lazy breeze. His gaze swept over her as he paused beside them.

"Hello, everyone," he said.

"Let's see what Lon's men have accomplished," Valerie said, tugging at his arm. "Come along. Let's have a closer look."

Cleve hesitated for a fraction of a second. "Are you two coming?"

"I'd like to show you around, Miss Tracy," Lon said politely.

"You must be busy —"

Lon smiled. "If the boss doesn't care, who am I to worry about it?"

Sondra found herself an unwilling member of the party. Lon explained about the project in an enthusiastic professional voice. During their conversation, she learned

he came from Dayton, Ohio, and that his parent company specialized in building lodges, hotels and other recreational areas from the ground up.

"All we need is a design and a plan of what the owner wants. We take care of everything else, hire the crews, get the materials, and oversee it until it's completed."

"It sounds like a fascinating job."

"Frustrating is a better word," Lon smiled. "At least at times. There are plenty of headaches to go with it, but I like the challenge."

Valerie and Cleve had moved ahead, Valerie bending her dark head close to Cleve's to talk with him, pointing out this and that. Now and then she could hear the murmur of Cleve's voice asking a question. He never looked back to Sondra, but she was aware of him, of the straight line of his shoulders, the way he stood, the turn of his head as he glanced here and there. Every movement was so achingly familiar.

"Where are you staying while you're here?" Lon asked.

She drew her attention back to the man beside her. "Half a mile away. At a cottage called Wild Willow."

"Then we're neighbors. I'm living at the Grandview."

Valerie and Cleve had started back toward them. Sondra did not want to speak with them again. She glanced at her watch.

"It's getting late. I must go. Thank you for the tour, Lon."

"If you're going back to Wild Willow, I'm going that way. I'll drop you off."

Sondra was glad that she need not meet Cleve's gray eyes again or hear his voice, or see how Valerie clung so possessively to his arm.

Lon's station wagon was crowded with blueprints,

briefcases and assorted building samples. He tossed them into the rear seat and helped her into the car.

Lon talked all the way to the cottage. Once there, he stretched his long, sunburned arm on the back of the seat and turned toward her.

"I just had a great idea. I go over to Antonio's nearly every night for dinner. Why don't you come with me tonight?"

"Antonio's!" she said with a smile. "My goodness, I haven't been there in ages."

"Then you'll come?"

"All right."

"Good! I'll pick you up at seven."

4

FROM THE Grandview Hotel, a young man stood at the window, looking out at the new clubhouse taking shape. He had just come in. He'd very nearly been caught a little while ago. But he lived on narrow escapes. All his life had been one big narrow escape. Next time he'd have to be more careful. He hadn't expected anyone to come into the cottage.

He lighted a cigarette and broke the match ruthlessly. There was just enough money in his pocket to pay for a week's lodging at the hotel and enough change to keep him in coffee and sandwiches. He was sick and tired of living like this, tired of being on the down side of the hill.

That's why it had to work. The whole scheme just *had* to work! He'd put in plenty of hours of hard thinking and planning, even when Gladys had been all against it.

"You got to reach out and take what you want in this world," he'd told her. "I'm tired of being nobody. I think it's time we changed all that. You going to back me up or not?"

"Sonny, I'm just not sure we can pull it off."

"What have we got to lose?" he said.

It had taken some doing to get her to agree. Without her he doubted he could make it stick. Gladys would be the clincher.

Now he was here and his nerves were taut with pent-up excitement. In a few days he'd make his first move. But before he did, he wanted to nose around and get the lay of the land, smell out the situation. He needed to know a few more things. He'd already made a start, even if it had been a bad one.

Tomorrow, he'd go into Lewiston. When it was all over they'd be in clover, he and Gladys. He laughed to himself. It was a hell of a good idea. He just wished he had thought of it years sooner. It would work. He *knew* it would.

He was hungry. He crushed out his cigarette and counted his money. It might even be necessary to take a job for a week or so to see him through. Maybe he could get something over at the construction site. A place like that ought to need an extra man.

There was a snack bar in the hotel off the lobby and he went down. He took a stool at the counter and ordered a sandwich and coffee.

"With plenty of cream," he said, eyeing the waitress. "What's your name, sweetie?"

She gave him a direct look. "I answer to Suzy. What's yours?"

"They call me Sonny."

She was sort of cute. Her skirt was just short enough to be enticing, her hair was black and long and her eyes were done up with lots of mascara in a real fancy way.

"You live around here?" he asked when she came with his coffee.

"Why do you ask?"

He gave her his most boyish grin. "Just making conversation. Is there a law against that?"

"I get my share of fresh ones in here," Suzy said tartly. "Old geezers that come here for the summer that suddenly have an attack of young blood. And salesmen, husbands on the prowl, you name it —"

"I'm not any of those, Suzy," Sonny said. "Honest. This is good coffee."

Suzy eyed him curiously. He gave her another smile and reached for a newspaper that had been left on the counter.

"That's yesterday's paper," she said.

"It's okay. I just wanted to look at the ads. Need a job. Know where I could get one?"

"Maybe over across the way. Never know."

"I thought about that. Thanks."

When she brought his sandwich, she lingered, giving him pensive looks. But he decided to ignore her. If he wanted a woman to get interested in him, a little indifference whetted her appetite. He usually played up to waitresses. Enough sweet talk and sometimes they'd accidentally forget to charge him for everything he'd eaten.

He thumbed half-heartedly through the want ads of the Lewiston paper while he ate his sandwich. Maybe he wouldn't even need the job if things went as planned and he could move fast enough.

"It's too risky," Gladys had kept saying. "We'll get tripped up. We don't need any more trouble."

"It will work, I tell you! All we have to do is plan it out and cover every possible angle."

He had been convinced and still was. He was about to toss the newspaper aside when his eye caught a certain

name in the obituary column. He froze. He read quickly and swore under his breath. He read the article a second time, just to be certain.

"Damn!" he said aloud.

Suzy looked around at him.

"Something wrong?"

"What? Oh, no, nothing," Sonny replied.

He was so angry his head was throbbing and his eyes burned. It was with supreme effort that he kept from wadding the paper and throwing it aside. But Suzy was still watching him.

They were too late! Why hadn't he got here quicker. Just a day or two would have made all the difference!

He couldn't finish his sandwich. He slapped the money on the counter and hurried out of the snack bar. He didn't care if Suzy was staring after him.

The minute he reached his room, he snatched the phone off the hook and put in a long distance call. He waited impatiently for Gladys to answer. Where was she? Why didn't she come on the line?

"Gladys!"

She was frightened. "What's happened. You're in jail, aren't you? It didn't work!"

"No. Listen. I haven't done anything yet. I told you I'd be a few days. But something's come up. I've hit a snag. I saw it in the paper."

"What are you talking about?"

"I'm afraid the whole deal's off."

He explained. On the other end of the line, Gladys was angry and disappointed too.

"Our luck!" she said bitterly.

"We missed a big one, Gladys."

He was about to hang up when it occurred to him in a flash that there were two ways to look at it.

"Hey, wait a minute, Gladys! Maybe this is to our advantage. Now, listen —"

They talked for several minutes, batting ideas back and forth, discussing the risks involved, and finally deciding it could very well be easier than ever to pull it off now.

Gladys saw the sense of it. "You're right, Sonny. I think this time you've got a chance."

He laughed gleefully and hung up. It *would* work! Who was there to dispute their word now? No one! Absolutely no one!

Cleve was not truly interested in seeing all the work that Lon and his men had done at the recreational area, but Valerie was insistent.

He saw Sondra leaving with Lon and frowned.

"I suppose you know why she's back in town," Valerie said.

"Carrie Winterhall was very special to Sondra," Cleve replied.

"I'd come back too, for all that money."

Cleve paused, staring at Valerie. "What do you mean?"

Valerie laughed and brushed back a lock of dark hair. "You mean you haven't heard? That's what you get for burying yourself out there in that musty old college."

"Lewiston College is not old or musty," he said. "Now what did you mean?"

"Daddy's attorney heard it through Quentin Hancock. Besides, it's a matter of public record down at the courthouse. Carrie left Sondra her entire estate."

Cleve strove to keep the surprise off his face. "I see."

"Strange about that, isn't it? I thought you were counting on fifty thousand for the college when the old lady died."

Cleve licked his lips. "Apparently Carrie changed her mind."

"Listen, if you'd be nice to Daddy, he'd give you the fifty thousand."

Cleve felt his face go warm. "Your father has already been most generous. I've learned in my job never to count on any endowments until they're in my hand. Honey, I must be getting back to the college. I've work to do."

"Oh, stay!" Valerie said impatiently. "I want to show you more of what's been done here."

"It's all very impressive and I'm sure it will be quite nice," Cleve said. "But I do have to go, Valerie."

"You haven't forgotten the party Saturday night, have you?"

"I told you, I can't come. Not this time. I have another appointment."

Valerie made a pretty face and clung to his arm. "Oh, I'll miss you so."

Cleve looked down into her lovely face. Valerie wrapped her arms around his neck and kissed him eagerly. Then he said good-bye and walked to his car.

"Call me," she shouted after him.

He was glad to drive away from the new clubhouse. He knew what plans Valerie had in the back of her mind. She had tried several times to discuss them with him. He'd even had a phone call from her father. But he hadn't budged, nor did he intend to. He had the utmost respect for Ed DeReuss, but he knew, too, that Ed had a tendency to steamroller his employees. Cleve wanted none of that. He had taken the job at the college as Financial

Coordinator because it had been a challenge, a job that he knew he could do well. Every day he saw Lewiston College changing, struggling to grow and keep up with the busy, hectic world. It was exciting to be a part of it.

"So, Carrie left her estate to Sondra," he murmured. "But then, why not?"

At first, the news had surprised him. But on the other hand, Carrie had loved Sondra. Sondra had filled a special need in Carrie's life. No one knew that better than he.

Still, why give it *all* to Sondra? Carrie was not the kind that went back on her word. He remembered very well the time he had spoken with her more than two years ago. She had phoned him at the college and asked him to drop by.

"At your convenience, Cleve," Carrie had told him.

"For you I'll come right away," he had replied.

He recalled going that very same day, sitting in her living room, the sunlight pouring through the windows. He had felt peaceful and happy there. It was before all the trouble with Sondra.

"I want to give you a check for the college," Carrie had told him.

She had written it out for him at the old-fashioned desk and pressed it into his hand.

"It's not a large one. But I hope it will help."

"It always helps," Cleve remembered telling her. "You've given the college a check every year for — how long?"

She smiled sadly. "Since Phillip went there years ago — and when I'm gone, Cleve, there will be more. A handsome sum. I've written it into my will."

"Bless you, Carrie," Cleve said. "It's people like you who make Lewiston College what it is."

She patted his hand with a maternal air. "I'm glad

you're working there, Cleve. You belong there."

"I think I do too, Carrie."

"And when are you going to steal my Sondra away and marry her?"

At that, he had laughed and bent down to leave a kiss on Carrie's cheek. "Soon, old dear. Soon!"

Now Cleve drove back to Lewiston, down the tree-lined streets and out to the college. He found his way into the administration building and to his office. He sat behind his desk, and in a small notebook where he'd made a list, he drew a line through Carrie's name. With a sigh, he slapped it shut. The legacy from Carrie would have been put to very good use. But now it wouldn't be coming.

He didn't begrudge Sondra a penny of the money. The girl deserved it. If love and attention and time had meant anything at all to Carrie, then Sondra certainly was entitled to Carrie's estate. But he was still puzzled. What had made Carrie change her mind about the gift to the college? Still, the old woman never did anything without a great deal of thought. She always knew what she was doing every step of the way.

"So why wonder about it?" Cleve asked himself. "It's the way she wanted it. I'm sure of that."

He leaned back in his chair and swiveled it so he could look out to the campus. It hadn't been so very long ago that he and Sondra —

He broke off his thoughts. That was over. Done. He had locked her out of his heart and mind and that was the way he must keep it.

5

Sondra spent the rest of the afternoon at Wild Willow unpacking. But she had no real heart for it. Finally, she took a stroll out to the dock, listening to her footsteps ringing out over the water. There was a board or two beginning to rot. She sidestepped them gingerly and went to the end of the landing and paused.

Across the lake, she could barely make out the red-tiled roof of Antonio's Restaurant. It was well known in the area and a favorite of many who visited the lake each summer. The restaurant was housed in an adobe-styled building with arched windows. Wine bottles were imbedded here and there in the outside walls so that the light shone through, dotting the interior with flashes of red, brown and green. Inside, there were several dining rooms with small tables and wood fireplaces that were kept burning, even in the summer.

"A ridiculous idea," Cleve used to say. "Heating the place with a fire and then cooling the whole business with air conditioning!"

"I think it's a marvelous idea!"

Cleve had smiled at her, gray eyes watching her with

their warm little lights. "I know. So do I. I was only teasing. Do you know how lovely you are by firelight?"

"Masher —" she said softly, laughing.

Sondra stirred, breaking her gaze away from Antonio's. Why did she keep remembering this sort of thing? It was all behind her, broken off, finished. She was almost sorry that she had agreed to go to Antonio's with Lon Greene.

When Lon's station wagon pulled up to the cottage a few minutes before seven, she was ready and waiting. Lon had changed to a light summer suit with a blue shirt and a bright tie. He was tall and attractive. He smiled when he saw her.

"You look great, Sondra. I called Antonio. He promised to save us a corner table."

Her heart did a flip-flop but she kept the smile on her face. Cleve had always asked for a corner table. Lon took her arm and walked with her to the car.

A short drive took them around to the other side of the lake. Antonio's looked dearly familiar and, with a wrench of emotion, Sondra walked inside. Antonio saw her at once.

He was a plump man with a black moustache, round cheeks and dancing dark eyes. He had pudgy hands and a large ruby on a little finger.

"Sondra!" he said.

He came rushing to her and he embraced her, kissing her on both cheeks, laughing and talking all at once. "How good to see you! It's been a long, long time!"

"Yes, it has, Antonio. Tell me, is your food as good as it used to be?"

"Better," he said, kissing her fingertips. "I've got a new

cook. The best yet. I didn't know you were going to be Mr. Greene's guest tonight."

"How is Maria?"

"My wife is fine. Fat and sassy. Just the way I like her," Antonio said with a wink. "Come, I'll show you to your table."

On the way to one of the small dining rooms, Antonio paused beside a shelf where several gold cups and trophies were displayed.

"See, I still have it!" Antonio said proudly.

She reached out to take the gold cup in both hands. She saw her name engraved there along with Cleve's.

"I'd nearly forgotten this."

"How could you do that?" Antonio exclaimed. "You were the best — the absolute best I've ever seen!"

"What is this?" Lon asked.

"I used to sponsor a dance contest for the young couples around the lake. Sondra and Cleve won a few years back. Never saw anyone do the Charleston as well," Antonio explained.

"The Charleston!" Lon asked with raised brows.

"Any period was eligible," Sondra explained. "I happen to like the Charleston, so —"

She put the cup back on the shelf.

"That seems a very long time ago, Antonio," she said.

"Not so long," Antonio said. "I was sorry to hear about Carrie."

Sondra nodded. "Yes. I-I haven't quite gotten used to the idea yet."

"And what about your mother, Sondra? I never hear anything about her any more. Did she come back too?"

Sondra shook her head quickly. "No. She didn't."

Sondra didn't want to talk about her mother. Nor think about her.

She was relieved to see that Antonio was putting them in the east room. She and Cleve had never come here. Their table had been in the opposite end of the building where they could look out at the lake.

Lon held the chair for her and Antonio snapped his fingers and motioned for one of his waiters to take care of them. He put a hand on Sondra's shoulder.

"Don't be a stranger," he said. "If I have time, I'll come back and we'll have a little visit —"

Then Antonio was gone, hurrying away to greet other guests. Across the table, Lon Greene was watching her.

"I didn't realize you and Antonio were such good friends."

"Antonio is everyone's friend. That's why everyone likes him so much."

"Wild Willow belonged to Carrie Winterhall, didn't it? I met her once after I first came here. She struck me as being a unique individual."

"She was that."

Lon studied the menu and asked what she would like to have. All her old favorites were still there. But she quickly decided against some of them. Somehow, she could not have lasagne and red wine with anyone but Cleve. She decided on an American dish. Lon ordered. Then he leaned back and gave her an appraising glance.

"Do you know Valerie and Cleve well?" he asked.

"They were in my crowd at college."

"Val's quite a girl."

"Oh, yes," Sondra nodded. "She always was."

"Do I detect a little something tart in your voice?" he asked with lifted brows.

"No," she shook her head quickly.

He laughed but said no more. She knew she had betrayed her feeling for Valerie without intending to. Lon Greene was perceptive and quick. She would do well to remember that.

"Tell me about Dayton," she said. "How did you get in this business of building recreational facilities?"

"Luck mostly. Aren't a lot of things luck? I have a degree in architecture. I worked for a construction company while I was in college. I got some down-to-earth knowledge that way. Combining the two — well, it just worked out. I like what I do."

"What about your family?"

"Two nice parents. One pretty sister, married, who has made me a proud uncle a couple of times. What about you? Antonio mentioned your mother."

Sondra kept a tight smile on her face.

"Mother's in the East. She works for an accounting firm there."

"And your father —"

"Dead. About a year ago."

"Oh, I'm sorry. I didn't know —"

"No brothers. No sisters. Sometimes I think I was cheated that way. I always wanted a sister."

"Tell me about L.A. and what you do there."

It was easier to talk about Imports, Inc., and her trips abroad. Lon was a good listener. He asked intelligent questions, and every now and then he would look at her with a quizzical expression on his face and say "Charleston!" and shake his head.

They laughed at that as they ate and the evening passed pleasantly. Antonio dropped by their table later and joined them for a few minutes. He tried to talk about

the past, but Sondra steered him in other directions. Instead they talked about the new golf course and the extra business it would probably bring Antonio.

"I've always got room for more. Now, Sondra, you come again. Anytime. I'll treat you to dinner for old times' sake."

"Thanks, Antonio, I'll remember that."

Lon seemed ready to make it a long evening. But Sondra was still tired from the long flight and the jarring homecoming.

"You'd better take me home, Lon. I'm getting fuzzy-headed and I'm sure I don't make much sense."

"All right. If you want."

They left Antonio's and stepped out into the clear, cool night. September was leading the way into autumn.

"The lake is very pretty this time of year," Lon said.

"But when the trees really begin to turn, it's lovelier still," Sondra said.

"I hope to have a big share of my work here done by then, before cold weather sets in."

"And then where will you go?"

"Back to Dayton, and from there — who knows?" Lon asked. "It could be anywhere."

"Do you like to be so unsettled?"

Lon laughed and took her arm as they walked to the car.

"It's the only way to go."

"That wouldn't be for me."

"Ah, you're a homebody, is that it?"

"I suppose that's as good a name as any," she said.

They drove away along the lake, seeing the water glinting in the starlight, hearing the sound of insects singing. The lake was unusually quiet, with only a faint breeze

stirring the treetops and rustling the leaves. They said very little until they reached Wild Willow and Lon walked with her to the door and unlocked it for her.

"This is a nice place. It looks so cozy."

"I love it here. I always have."

Lon took her hand for a moment in his. "I'll see you again, Sondra. This has been fun. I'll phone."

He didn't wait for her to say whether or not it would be all right. But before he reached his car he turned back with a laugh. "Charleston!"

She smiled and waved. Then she went inside the empty cottage and turned on the lights.

She did not sleep well that night. Perhaps she was still too tired, or perhaps it was the quiet. It was so different from busy, noisy Los Angeles. She had forgotten what it was like to hear a screech owl in the middle of the night and leaves brushing her window.

There was no food in the cottage, a condition she must remedy. But she carried a jar of instant coffee with her when she traveled abroad and she made several cups for her breakfast.

Sometime she would have to contact Mrs. Fulton and arrange for her to continue looking after the cottage, and someone would have to be hired to do some work outside. That and a dozen other things. She would be meeting Maxine Davis from Webb and Company within an hour and she was anxious to get things moving.

A few minutes later she went outside, got in her car and started to back out of the drive. The radio was blaring with music, and perhaps it was this or simply that she had her mind elsewhere. She was halfway out into the road when she heard another car coming. She slammed on her brakes, but it was too late.

There was a crash as they collided, the sound of metal grinding against metal. She was pitched forward and her forehead struck the windshield. She shook her head to clear it, but the blackness kept persisting.

Somehow, she got the door open, but her legs were like butter. Two big arms caught her and she saw a pair of alarmed eyes looking out of a big face. The man was wearing a yellow hard hat with the stenciled name R. Wagner across the front of it. She remembered that much as well as the sound of his voice just before she blacked out.

6

W HEN SONDRA opened her eyes, she saw pale green walls and heard a phone ringing. Then slowly she turned her head and saw a tray of medicines and bandages and then Gretta leaned over her, her gray eyes studying her seriously.

"Welcome back," Gretta said with a smile. "How do you feel?"

"Is this your office?"

"Yes."

"What happened?"

"Don't you remember?" Gretta asked.

"All I know right now is that I've got a headache."

She reached up to touch her forehead and found a bandage.

"Easy. You've got a small cut and a nasty bruise," Gretta said.

"I was leaving Wild Willow," Sondra said, things beginning to come back. "I remember now! There was an accident. Someone ran into my car just as I was backing out of the driveway."

"That someone's out in my reception room pacing a

hole in the carpet," Gretta said with a smile. "Any blurring of vision?"

"A little."

"Do you feel dizzy?"

"I-I don't know. I just feel a little peculiar."

Gretta leaned over her again, feeling behind her ears, pressing against the back of her head. Sondra lay quietly trying to clear her thoughts, looking around at Gretta's neat examining room.

"How did I get here?" she asked.

"In the arms of an attractive man," Gretta smiled. "I don't know how you manage it, Sondra. You never do anything unless it's with style."

"I remember. The man with the bulldozer! The one that tore our house down. R. Wagner. I *hate* that man!"

"Easy," Gretta said. "Lie still for another minute or two. I've not finished."

"Is all of this necessary?" Sondra asked, watching Gretta as she prepared to take her blood pressure.

"Very necessary," Gretta smiled. "What's the matter, doesn't my bedside manner please you?"

Sondra managed a short laugh. "I simply can't get used to this — you being my doctor."

"Be still now. Let me finish and maybe I'll let you out of here."

She watched Gretta's capable hands as she went about her work.

"Sit up now, please. Let's see how you feel?"

Gretta helped her sit on the edge of the examination table. The room went around and around for a moment but gradually righted itself.

"Okay?" Gretta asked.

"Yes, I think so. But I just remembered! I was on my

way to Carrie's house. I have an appointment with Maxine Davis this morning. What time is it?"

"About ten."

"Be a lamb, will you, and phone Maxine's office? Perhaps we can catch her before she leaves. Ask her to meet me at the house tomorrow instead."

Gretta made the call, spoke with Maxine and made the appointment for the next day.

"Thanks, Gretta."

"All part of my service," Gretta said. "All right, on your feet. If you feel faint, tell me."

But she was solid enough as she stood up and Gretta seemed satisfied.

"Wait here. Mr. Wagner wants to see you."

"I don't want to see him —" Sondra called after her. But Gretta had gone. In a moment, R. Wagner appeared in the room, hard hat in his hand.

"The doctor says you're going to be all right, Miss Tracy."

"I think I'll live," she said wryly. "No thanks to you. What kind of a war are you waging against me? First my house, then my car —"

R. Wagner flushed. "Sorry. I really *am* sorry, Miss Tracy. But you came tearing out of that driveway so fast and you didn't look or you would have seen me."

"What about my car?"

"Well, the left side is pretty well smashed in. But my insurance will take care of it."

"It was a rented car."

"I'll talk to the rental company," he said. "You're not to worry about it, Miss Tracy."

He stood uneasily, rubbing a nervous hand over his dark curly hair. His brown eyes kept watching her anx-

iously. He was dressed neatly in matched work clothes and heavy boots.

"I'll go down there right now and explain what happened. I'll arrange for them to bring a new car here for you. Okay?" he asked.

He was fingering the hard hat nervously, waiting for her to reply. She pointed to it.

"What does the R stand for?"

"Russ," he said. "Russ Wagner. I was on my way to the new clubhouse when we collided. I've got three of my men doing some work there."

"Do you own that string of bulldozers that has been clearing out the houses for the freeway?"

"Yes, I do. Listen, is there anything else I can do for you, Miss Tracy?"

"I think you've done quite enough already!" Sondra replied with an edge in her voice.

He flushed again and said he'd be going.

"I'll take care of everything," he said. "You're not to worry."

Then he rushed out to the hall where Sondra saw him conferring with Gretta. At last he was gone. Gretta came back into the room.

"He's very upset," Gretta said. "He told me three times that he'd take care of the bill. How's your head now?"

"It still aches."

"I've got to drive over to Newberry for a consultation this morning. Why don't you come along?"

"Thanks, Gretta, but you don't need to coddle me."

"You're certain you feel up to going home?" Gretta asked anxiously.

"I've got a dozen things to do."

"My advice is to forget them. Have a long nap and get some fresh air. Doctor's orders."

She laughed. "You make it sound inviting."

"Weren't you being a little hard on Mr. Wagner a few minutes ago?"

"I don't like him," Sondra stated flatly.

Gretta gave her a knowing look. "It's not his fault that he had to tear your old house down."

"Why didn't you tell me about that? Why did you just let me go there yesterday and find it gone?"

Gretta lifted her shoulders in a sigh. "I couldn't bring myself to tell you. I knew how you'd react. I tried several times to write you about it. I should have. I had no idea you would be coming to Lewiston unexpectedly. Am I forgiven?"

Sondra eyed her old friend and then gave her a nod. "Oh, you know I couldn't stay angry with you if I tried!"

Gretta poured a dozen white tablets into a small envelope and handed them to her. "One every four hours until your headache leaves. If it doesn't, call me."

Sondra took them and tucked them into her purse. "All right, Doctor. As you say. Why don't you come to Wild Willow for dinner tonight? Nothing fancy, mind you, but I'll fix something. You used to love it out there."

"I still do. All right. If you'll promise to rest this afternoon and won't fuss with a big meal, I'll come."

"Good! I'll expect you. And thanks, hon, for everything."

Gretta gave her a warm smile. She was such a small woman, so frail. How could she endure the hard rigors of a doctor's life? Still, Sondra knew that Gretta had hidden strength. More than once, she had leaned against that

strength herself. It was always Gretta who had the common sense answers, who could get down to the core of matters, put things into their proper places.

When the new car was delivered, Sondra made a stop at the supermarket. There was one other errand she wanted to do on the way home. If she took the long way around the lake, she could stop by and see Mrs. Fulton about continuing to keep the cottage clean for her.

The lake was so bright in the sunlight, it hurt her eyes. Her head was still throbbing and the thought of sleeping in a hammock in the shade of one of the trees at Wild Willow became more tempting by the minute.

Mrs. Fulton lived in a small frame house on the west side of the lake and she was at home, rocking on the front porch, a piece of sewing in her lap. Mrs. Fulton stared as the strange car came to a stop.

"Hello, Mrs. Fulton. Remember me?"

"Of course I do. Sondra Tracy. Heard you were back."

Sondra went up to the porch and because her legs still felt shaky, she sat down on the steps.

"I know you've been taking care of Wild Willow for Carrie, Mrs. Fulton. I'd like for you to keep on doing it for me."

Mrs. Fulton rocked for a moment, minding her sewing with infinite care.

"I've been thinking of cutting down on my work. Got so many places to care for," she said stiffly.

Sondra hid a frown. She knew what Mrs. Fulton wanted. It annoyed her and yet amused her at the same time. By now she was certain the amount of inheritance she had been given by Carrie had reached outrageous proportions on the gossip grapevine.

"I could give you another five dollars a week, if you'd be interested, Mrs. Fulton."

Mrs. Fulton looked at her. "Ten and I'll consider it."

Sondra sighed. "All right, ten."

"I'll be there in the morning," Mrs. Fulton said.

"Good. You have a key. I'll be busy in town, but I'll expect you."

Sondra got up to leave and had walked halfway to her car when she turned back with a thought.

"By the way, Mrs. Fulton, did you happen to be there yesterday afternoon? Did you leave by the front way just as I was coming in the back?"

Mrs. Fulton looked up sharply. "Haven't put foot inside the place since Carrie took sick so sudden and went to the hospital. Didn't figure it was any of my business to be there."

"I see," Sondra said thoughtfully. "Thank you."

She didn't believe that Mrs. Fulton was lying. But she couldn't shake the feeling that she had nearly surprised someone inside. Still, nerves could do strange things, and she'd been weary to the bone and her emotions wrought up.

She drove on to the cottage, put the groceries away in the cupboard and took Gretta's advice. She napped for more than three hours, sleeping right through lunchtime and into the middle of the afternoon.

It was fun to prepare dinner for Gretta. She anticipated talking with her old friend over a leisurely meal. By the time the Swiss steak was baked to perfection, the sun was sinking toward the horizon. The lake seemed very calm and only a few boats were still out on the peaceful water.

Gretta came a few minutes later and sniffed the air hungrily.

"I'm starved. What smells so good?"

"Swiss steak."

"You remembered!"

"Of course. Sit down. You look tired. You must have had a busy day."

"Very. I gave my answering service your number here. But with luck, we'll not be interrupted."

"How do you stand it? Being on call all hours of the day and night?"

Gretta sat down at the table and looked out to the lake. "It's part of being a doctor."

Sondra served them and sat down opposite her friend. They talked about Gretta's work for a while and then the conversation swung to Sondra.

"I assume this superb meal means that you're feeling all right," Gretta said. They laughed together.

"You know, it's not the first time I've had to take care of you," Gretta added. "Remember that time when we were kids and you took a spill on your bike? I thought surely you'd broken a leg."

"Do I remember! I still have the scars."

"We've had so many marvelous times together," Gretta said. "It was a wrench for me too when I found your old house was gone."

Sondra looked away, not wanting to remember the bleakness she had felt when she'd found the house had been destroyed.

"Your place was my second home," Gretta said. "Oh, I loved going there! It was so different at your house than at mine."

Sondra reached over to cover Gretta's small hand for a moment. "I know. Things were never easy for you."

"But what I lacked at home, I found at your house," Gretta said. "Your parents were so kind to me. Especially your mother —"

Sondra drew her hand quickly away.

"What about her, Sondra?" Gretta asked.

"She still has her job and I expect her to be married to her boss any day now."

"Is she happy?"

"I'm sure of it!" Sondra replied.

"Are things any better between you now?"

"Not really."

Gretta flashed her a look of despair. "Oh, Sondra, can't you forgive her?"

Sondra looked away. "No."

"There are two sides to everything, you know."

"I don't want to talk about it, Gretta!"

"I know you were terribly hurt. I understand that, but it's over, done —"

Sondra clenched her hands tightly together.

"I can't forget it, Gretta."

"But look what you've let it cost you! Your mother, Cleve, even leaving Lewiston, a town I know you love! Sondra, you've got a level head on your shoulders. You're a very intelligent woman. How can you —"

"None of it made sense. Not one thing Mother did made any sense!"

Gretta got up to pour them another cup of coffee. She put a hand for a moment on Sondra's rigid shoulder.

"Sondra, Helen Tracy never did anything without a reason. I knew her too well. But I shouldn't rake up cold ashes, should I? Forgive me. I just thought by now that perhaps you had mellowed, softened a little —"

Sondra couldn't reply to that. It was possible she *had* softened to a degree. But there was still a wall between her and her mother.

They drank the last of the coffee in companionable silence, watching the last of the sun sink out of sight, seeing the reflections on the water change from red to pink to lavender and then into darkness.

The cottage grew shadowy and Sondra went to turn on the lamps.

"What are you going to do about Cleve?" Gretta asked.

Sondra spun around to stare at her friend. "What do you mean? What is there to do? I went my way, Cleve went his."

"You still love him, don't you?"

"No comment," Sondra said.

Gretta sighed and shook her head. "You two! So much alike! So stubborn and foolish."

"You told me yourself that Cleve was interested in Valerie DeReuss and I saw that for myself yesterday."

"It's not going to work with Valerie and Cleve."

"Why on earth do you make a statement like that?"

"Simple," Gretta said. "I know Cleve. He's stubborn and full of male pride, but deep down, Sondra, I don't think he ever got over you."

7

LONG AFTER Gretta had gone, her words rang in Sondra's ears. But this time she knew her old friend was wrong. Cleve did not forgive or forget easily. Their parting had been bitter and angry. No, Cleve had long since put her into the past, forgotten her. Valerie DeReuss was proof of that.

The next morning, Sondra was reluctant to keep her appointment with Maxine Davis at Carrie's house, but she knew she must. The quicker she got the ball rolling, the quicker she could go back to Los Angeles where she belonged.

The Saturday sun was bright and warm, even though the air had turned cooler in the night. Sondra drove straight to Carrie's house and saw that Maxine Davis was already there, waiting for her.

Maxine was a short woman with a figure going plump, thick, dark hair stylishly done and an efficient air about her. When they stepped inside the house, she looked around with knowing eyes.

"You've got some wonderful antiques!" she said. "Will you be selling them?"

"I don't know. But that decision doesn't have to be made yet. I need a list of what is here. How long do you think it will take you to make it?"

"Several days," Maxine said. "The dishes alone will take quite a while."

"Will you be able to start immediately?"

"I'll plan to start Monday, if that's agreeable with you. I seldom work past noon on Saturdays and I would barely get a start now."

"I see. All right, then. Monday."

Sondra could see that she was going to be held up here for some time. Perhaps the wise thing to do would be to return to Los Angeles, leave the house in Maxine's hands, and come back later. But somehow she didn't want to do that.

Carrie had an old-fashioned, pigeon-hole desk. Sondra had seen her sitting there so many times.

"My husband gave me this," Carrie had told her once, "as a wedding gift."

There was one compartment that locked and Sondra knew where the key was kept. Once she had seen Carrie open it and look for a long while at a newspaper clipping she kept there. She'd been curious and had even asked about it, but it was one of the few times Carrie had not given her an answer.

Remembering it now, Sondra searched the desk until she found the key, unlocked it and reached inside. The envelope was old and yellowed. It had been handled many times. She turned the contents out onto the top of the desk. There was a small photo. Sondra looked into the handsome face of a young man.

"Phillip," Sondra murmured. "Carrie's son."

He had been a rakish devil. What little she knew about

him had come down in the form of gossip from the neighbors. She knew Phillip had been quite the man about town and had had an eye for the girls. He had fallen into disfavor with his father, a stern, old-fashioned sort of man, and because of this they had quarreled bitterly. As a result, Phillip had left home. To Sondra's knowledge, he had never come back or even kept in touch with his parents. Carrie had spoken of him so seldom, but when she had it had been with a wistful loneliness in her voice.

Sondra remembered one time when she had asked about Phillip, daring to open a subject which she knew was sensitive. But she had never forgotten Carrie's answer.

"My husband and Phillip didn't get along. I'm afraid Kermit never truly tried to understand our son. I was softer, you know how it is with mothers. I loved Phillip, no matter what. But he went away and he never came back."

"How terrible!"

Carrie had not replied to that, but Sondra remembered the tears that came to her eyes, the way she had turned away to hide them. Sondra had been at a very tender age then, all of fifteen, and her head spun with the drama of it all. She had put her arms around Carrie and they stood that way for a moment or two, clinging to each other. Then the moment passed and they never spoke of Phillip again. But the incident had stayed inside Sondra's heart.

Now she stared into the dark eyes of Phillip Winterhall in the photo and studied his face for a moment. He surely had not been like Carrie or he would not have been so cruel as never to have written or come home again.

Along with the photo, Sondra found the clipping she remembered seeing Carrie reading. It was a newspaper

photo of Phillip and his bride, Tonya. It was an announcement of their marriage in Philadelphia. How Carrie had come by the clipping, Sondra didn't know.

Tonya was a pretty girl with wide, clear eyes and dark hair curling around her face in the style of the day. The clipping gave little information.

There was one more item. The telegram was faded and had been handled so much it was nearly falling to pieces. The message was terse and heart-wrenching.

"Phillip died suddenly of heart attack last night." It was signed "Tonya."

The date on it proved that Phillip and Tonya had probably been married only a few months at the most.

Somehow Carrie's life seemed to be enclosed in this one worn envelope. Phillip had gone from home, married, died shortly afterward. But what about the grandson? This question plagued Sondra. She couldn't remember when she had first known there might be a grandson. Had Carrie said something to her? Or had she heard it in the neighborhood?

Carefully, Sondra put the two clippings and the photograph into a fresh envelope and tucked it into her purse for safekeeping. She knew she should stay at the house and decide about a few things, but she couldn't bring herself to do it.

She went back to spend a quiet afternoon at the lake cottage. The weather was balmy with the feel of Indian summer. She fixed herself a late lunch and sat at the window, watching the busy water-skiers on the lake.

Over a last cup of coffee, she peered once again at the photo of Phillip Winterhall and his bride, Tonya. Had there been a son born to them? If he lived, where was he?

Whom could she ask? Quentin Hancock said he knew nothing about a grandson. Who else in Lewiston might possibly know? Who else would Carrie have confided in?

"Nona!" Sondra exclaimed aloud. "Of course. Nona Campbell."

How could she have forgotten about Nona? Was she still living in that little house on Adams Street?

Sondra rushed to find the phone directory and looked up Nona's name. The address was the same. She slapped the book shut with a triumphant gesture. If anyone knew, it would be Nona.

She decided on the spot to pay the old lady a visit. She left the cottage and drove back to Lewiston. By the time she found her way to Adams Street, it was about three o'clock.

Nona's house was tidy but getting a little shabby now. Sondra knocked several times and was about to give up when she heard the tapping of a cane.

"Who is it?"

"Nona, it's Sondra Tracy. Do you remember me? Carrie's friend."

Nona unlocked the door and pulled it open a crack to peer out at her. Nona's hair was snow white and pulled back into a bun at the nape of her neck. She wore extremely thick glasses and she cocked her head in a manner that told Sondra her hearing was bad too.

"Could I talk to you for a little while, Nona?" Sondra asked.

"Yes. Yes, come in," Nona said, sounding pleased. "I don't have many visitors these days."

"How are you, Nona?"

Nona gave her a saucy grin. "Gettin' old and creaky, but I'm here."

"Are you still living alone?"

Nona laughed. "Aim to until they take me out of here feet first," she said. Then her laughter died away. "You know about poor Carrie?"

"Yes. That's why I'm here, Nona. I'd like to talk to you about her. I know you were close friends for many years."

"We go back a way," Nona nodded. "We were girlhood friends. Been friends all our lives, even if Carrie did marry a rich man and I married a poor one. Didn't make any difference to Carrie."

Sondra smiled. "I know. Nona, I'd like to know about Carrie's son, Phillip."

Nona sat down slowly in a worn rocker and tapped the floor with her cane. "Why, Phillip's dead. Been dead a long time. That rascal broke poor Carrie's heart."

"I understand he married out East."

"Yes."

"To a girl named Tonya Barrett. Do you remember that?"

"Not likely to forget it," Nona said, making a face. "She was a wild thing. Carrie never approved of her. Those Barretts were a wild bunch, the whole lot of them."

Sondra drew a deep breath, almost afraid to voice the next question. "Did Carrie ever tell you about her grandson?"

The rocker stopped. For a moment, the cane was poised above the floor. Then Nona pursed her lips and began rocking again a bit faster this time.

"Wasn't any grandson!"

Sondra leaned closer. "Nona, are you certain of that? It's very important that I know."

"There was no grandson! Carrie had no grandson, I tell you!" Nona said, her voice stern and severe. "Now, tell

me about you. Where have you been? Went to Los
Angeles, didn't you? I believe that's what Carrie told me."

Nona had changed the subject so abruptly that Sondra
was immediately suspicious. She watched the old woman
with her eyes huge and keen behind the thick glasses and
saw the firm way she clutched her cane. Sondra knew that
Nona had taken her stand. Perhaps it was something
Carrie had asked her to do, but Sondra knew instinctively
that Nona Campbell was hiding something. But why?

8

CLEVE RIDGEWAY lived at the Hotel Lewiston in a small apartment with a commanding view of the city. He never tired of looking out to the Mississippi River and the bluffs that rose above it.

He had a few hours' work at the college he wanted to do, even though it was Saturday. Classes were to begin next week, which made for extra work in all departments.

It took supreme concentration today to do his work. He found his mind wandering. Right this minute he wished he could leave the college and go home, get Pop and head for the duck blind. The blind was just an old shack on the river front where Pop used to wait for the ducks at dawn. Cleve had never shared his father's love of hunting, but he'd enjoyed the crisp mornings with fog shrouding above the water, the smell of coffee from the thermos and the warmth of the old kerosene burner that kept their feet from freezing.

Best of all, it was just being with Pop. True, he didn't have time to go home often these days. But in his mind, he went there nearly every day.

It was an unusually busy Saturday morning and, to top

it all, Valerie phoned, insisting she meet him for lunch at the hotel. "It's not pleasure, darling," she'd said. "It's business."

He had known Valerie ever since college days. She had been in their crowd. But then he had been aware only of Sondra Tracy and no one else. Strange how things worked out. Valerie had been just a pretty girl, someone he scarcely gave a second glance. Now all of that had changed.

He left his office and went back to the hotel. He much preferred the informal coffee shop, but Valerie had been explicit that she would meet him in the main dining room.

She sat prettily at a center table. Unlike most people who always hugged the walls and requested tables there, Valerie liked to be in the middle of the room. He knew it was deliberate. Everyone was sure to notice her there. She reached out and caught his hand for a moment and raised it to her lips. "Hello, darling."

"Have you been waiting long?"

"No. But you're late."

"Sorry. It's been a busy morning. What would you like?"

"You," she said with a smile. "For the afternoon."

"That's impossible."

Cleve took care of the order and held a match to Valerie's cigarette. Every move she made was as practiced and lovely as one made by a ballet dancer.

"What's so urgent?" he asked.

"You know my pet project is not going well. Lon is a full three weeks behind schedule."

"Blame it on a wet summer," he said.

"I've already heard that excuse," Valerie said. "I want

something better than that. I want answers. I want to see them catch up and meet the deadline."

"And what am I to do about that?" Cleve asked.

She put a hand on his sleeve. "Talk to Lon for me, darling. Man to man."

He smiled. "But this is *your* project," he reminded her. "You badgered your father into letting you do this —"

She smiled uneasily. "And that's why I want you to help me, Cleve. Dad will never let me live it down if things don't go well. Please, help me. Give Lon a dressing down for me."

Cleve frowned and reached into his pocket for his pipe. He fingered it for a moment, wishing he could fill it and light it, but Valerie didn't like the pipe, so he put it back in his pocket.

"Don't you think that you —"

"No, I want you to do it!"

"Asking or demanding?" he said wryly.

She lifted her brows and looked at him. He hated this streak in her, and whenever it surfaced he crushed it down.

"I didn't mean it like that, Cleve! I'd really like you to speak to Lon about it. Please?"

He took a deep breath. He might as well agree or she would badger him forever about it.

"All right. I'll try to talk to Lon in the next day or so. Will that do?"

She was all sunshine now. She beamed at him and he was struck by her loveliness.

"You're so sweet, Cleve."

"Just don't get the idea I'm your little errand boy, because I'm not."

"My, my, what a wounded male ego we have on our hands!"

He flushed. Then she laughed and tried to pass it off as if it had never been said. He knew what was behind the remark. She was angry because he wouldn't bend to her every wish, especially where her father was concerned. Valerie wanted him safely under Ed DeReuss's wing and she had no intention of letting him forget it.

She set about the rest of the lunch charming him, and Valerie was a woman who knew how to do that. She could change right before his eyes, showing a different phase of her personality with every breath.

When they finished eating, Valerie kissed him lightly and made him promise to phone her as soon as he had talked with Lon Greene.

"Are you sure you won't come to the house tonight?" she asked.

"I'm sure. Enjoy your party."

"I think you're being stubborn."

He gave her a quick look. "I have other plans."

"I'll miss you, Cleve."

Cleve returned to his office and handled a few minor problems awaiting him there. It was about four before he was able to leave.

He had planned for more than a week to drop in on his father today. He made his way through the city traffic and to the older section of town. The house had been the same for years and his father had done little to it since Cleve's mother had died except keep it neat and trim. It was a comfortable place and adequate for his father's needs.

Cleve left his car in the driveway and went to the back

door. He opened the screen door and stuck his head inside. "Hey, Pop!"

"Out here, son."

Mr. Ridgeway appeared in the doorway of the garage, a wrench in his hand, a greasy smudge on his face.

"What are you doing?" Cleve smiled.

"Fixing the lawn mower."

"Need some help?"

"You'll get your fancy suit all dirty and ruin your shirt."

"Doubt it," Cleve said. "What's wrong with the mower?"

"Beats me."

Mr. Ridgeway was in his late fifties and worked as a truck dispatcher at Arrow Lines. Cleve was a little taller but had the same basic frame as his father and the resemblance was strong. Mr. Ridgeway's hair was as thick and black but had touches of gray and his shoulders were beginning to stoop.

"Like two peas in a pod," his mother had often said about them.

Cleve stepped into the garage where his father had built a workbench. The mower was half torn down.

"Want the carburetor taken off?" he asked.

"That's what I had in mind."

Cleve bent to the task, shirt-sleeves rolled, necktie off and stuffed in his pocket.

"How's things at the college?"

"Like always. Busy. How's your job?"

His father shrugged. "Same old sixes and sevens. Planned on going fishing today, but got involved with this. How's Valerie?"

Cleve looked up. He had brought Valerie here just

once to meet his father. The encounter had been cool and Valerie had been at her snobbish worst.

"Okay, I suppose. Pop —"

"Yeah?"

"Sondra's back in town."

Mr. Ridgeway stopped working long enough to give him a quick look. "I heard."

"I keep running into her —"

"Should never have let her get away," he said. "It was the biggest mistake of your life."

Cleve straightened. "You always did side with her!"

"And you were always stubborn. Don't know where you got that streak — must have been from your mother's side."

"Let's just work on the mower," Cleve said with an edge in his voice.

"You brought up the subject, not me."

"I did, didn't I? The thing is — what do I do about it?"

Mr. Ridgeway tossed his wrench to the workbench.

"Now who am I to tell you that? Some things you have to decide for yourself, Cleve. I had a notion it was all over. Isn't that what you told me two years ago when Sondra left Lewiston?"

Cleve nodded. "Yes."

"Are you saying now that you've changed your mind?"

Cleve set his jaw. "No!"

"Then why in thunder are we talking about it?"

Cleve twisted a wrench too hard, too fast, and skinned his knuckle. He swore. He felt better.

"What do you say, shall we just ditch the mower and go fishing?"

Cleve managed a grin. "No, not today, Pop. If you want to go, go ahead. I'll stay and fix this."

"Like to get your hands dirty once in a while, don't you?"

Cleve nodded. "It gets me back to basics. I need it."

"Yeah, I know. You'll stay for supper, won't you?"

"Sure."

They didn't talk any more about Sondra, of fishing or anything but the mower, arguing good-naturedly about what was wrong with it, at times nearly losing their tempers when it failed to respond to their tinkering. But slowly, gradually, Cleve knew he was relaxing. He felt settled and sure of himself again.

Later they ate a simple supper and then sat on the porch, smoking their pipes.

Cleve hated the thought of returning to his apartment. But the restlessness he'd been feeling lately plagued him here too. As the night fell, the uneasiness deepened until he got to his feet with a rush.

"I'd better go," Cleve said.

"It's still early."

"I've got an errand to run. I'll see you soon, Pop."

Cleve started his car, waved good-bye and drove away. He had fully intended to stop by the Grandview Hotel and look up Lon Greene. But Saturday night was a bad time and Lon would probably be out.

But despite his decision to let it wait, he found himself driving out toward Reynolds Lake anyway. When he reached the fork in the road, he stopped. Then with a twist of the wheel, he turned right. He drove a short distance until Wild Willow came into sight. A light burned in the window. She was home.

Maybe it was habit, or some strange curiosity, or even a

kind of longing that made him turn in at the drive. He shut off the motor. He had his hand on the handle, ready to open the door and walk up the steps to knock.

Then his good sense came back to him. With an angry motion he twisted the key, the motor fired and he hurried away, driving very fast.

He didn't begin to breathe easier until he saw the lights of Lewiston, until he put the car in the hotel garage and went to his apartment. Going out to Wild Willow had been pure madness. They had nothing to say to each other.

9

Sunday was bright and the lake was buzzing with activity. From the hotel window, Sonny watched and frowned. He wished he had the money to rent a boat and take a long ride. The room was stale with cigarette smoke and littered with wadded pieces of paper where he had doodled by the hour, tying the last pieces all together in his head. By now, he had memorized everything he was sure he would need to know.

He was tempted to start the ball rolling right away, maybe even tomorrow morning. But he knew the thing to do was to proceed slowly. There were too many angles yet to cover. He was too close to blow it now.

He lighted his last cigarette and crumpled the package. His money was running low. Before he could do much of anything, he would have to put his hands on some hard cash. There was a likely place or two around, but he couldn't afford to risk it now. There was too much at stake. While it would be much simpler just to steal the money he needed, he knew he'd better play it straight this time. He'd get a job somewhere.

When the phone rang, he nearly jumped out of his

skin. He snatched up the receiver and answered cautiously.

"Sonny?"

"Gladys! What do you want? You haven't got cold feet on me, have you?"

"Not a chance. I'm in town. At the bus station."

"You're what?" he roared.

"I need a place to stay."

"What are you doing here? That wasn't in the plan at all. You were to stay right there at home until I called you. You'll foul up things for sure!"

"I won't. When are you going to do something? Tomorrow? Let's not wait."

"No!" he shouted.

He reminded himself that the walls of the hotel were thin and made himself quiet down.

"I've got a few things to check out first," he said. "I'm not ready. Now listen, you just turn right around and catch the next bus home."

"That would be stupid."

Sonny sighed and ran his hand over his hair, exasperated and impatient.

"I'm broke. Have you got any money?" he asked.

"Twenty dollars."

"How do you expect to get by on twenty dollars?"

"I'll soon be rich, won't I?"

Sonny licked his dry lips, "It's going to take time. I told you that —"

"All right. Slow down. I'll get a temporary job. I'll get along."

"Okay. Okay! But I don't want to be seen with you. Not just yet. You understand?"

She argued and they had a good row on the phone. But Sonny won out.

"I'll let you know where I'm staying," Gladys said.

Sonny hung up with a slam of the receiver. Leave it to a woman to put a snarl in things!

He managed to calm down at last and left his room in the middle of the afternoon. He drove to Lewiston, up one street and down another, familiarizing himself with the locale. He had supper at a drive-in and then he sat for a while in a small park overlooking the river, waiting for night.

When he was satisfied that it was dark enough, he drove away. He parked the car on a side street several blocks from the house and then went on foot, slipping down the alley and weaving an erratic pattern. When he had reached the place at last, he approached it from the rear, cautiously, pausing now and then to look around. Silently, he crossed the back porch and, taking a small tool kit from his pocket, he bent to his task. It took him only a moment or two to open the lock and step inside.

He was breathing heavily. He waited for a full second and heard nothing.

"It's okay," he muttered aloud. "I'm home free."

The first thing he did was pull the shades. Then, risking only a very small flashlight, he began looking around. He was disappointed, to say the least. It was not at all what he had expected. It was supposed to have been so grand. But he found it old-fashioned and sort of ugly.

He paced about the house, examining several rooms. Then he decided he had been there long enough. It was better to make these excursions short.

He snapped off his light and put the shades back the way he had found them. As he started to let himself out

the way he had come in, he heard something. Was it a key in the lock?

There were several things he could do — find a hiding place, try to slip out the front way, or grab something and lay in wait. Who else could be coming like this, slipping in quietly the back way? If someone else was butting in on the deal, he'd better find out who it was!

He crept close to the back door, crouched in the darkness, his hand closing around the barrel of his pistol. One quick, swift movement and somebody was going to wake up with a splitting headache.

The door was open now. Sonny drew a deep breath and poised, muscles straining, nerves jumping. A shadow slipped inside, the door latched and Sonny leaped.

There was a scream. A woman's scream. Gladys!

"Sonny? Is that you, Sonny?"

"I nearly creamed you!" Sonny said angrily. "Why didn't you stay put and let me handle this?"

"I just got curious, that's all."

Sonny grabbed her by the arm and pushed her roughly through the door and made sure the lock was latched behind them. Then he hustled her away from the house and into the safety of the dark alley.

"No more of this, do you hear?" he asked.

He couldn't see her face but he could see her lift her shoulders in a shrug.

"You're forgetting I taught you everything you know. I can still pick a lock better than you."

Suddenly Sonny saw the humor of it. "You know, you're right about that. Okay. I'll overlook it this time. But promise, leave it to me from here on in. When it's time for you to make your move, I'll let you know."

"All right, Sonny. I reckon you do know best."

"Did you get a room?"

"If you can call it that. But the landlady told me a place or two where I might get work."

Sonny, in a rare show of affection, put his arm around Gladys's scrawny shoulders.

"Won't be long you'll never have to work again. This time, our luck's going to change. Wait and see!"

It was late Monday afternoon when Cleve found some slack time and decided to drive out to talk with Lon Greene. Valerie would give him no rest until he'd done it.

It was a bright, sunshiny day. Cleve saw that Lon had a full crew going. They were pushing hard to meet the deadline. What more could Valerie want?

As Cleve went to find Lon, he paused for a moment to watch the work. It was hot in the sun. He peeled off his coat and loosened his tie. At the trailer where he kept his office, Lon was on the phone and angry about something. He hung up with a slam of the receiver.

"Problems?" Cleve asked.

Lon nodded. "And how! Nothing's gone right all day long!"

Lon was in a bad temper. Cleve knew it was not a good time to talk to him, but he'd already told Valerie he intended to come out today.

"Is this a social visit?" Lon asked.

Cleve filled his pipe and lighted it, tossing the dead match to an ashtray. "Afraid not, Lon. Valerie sent me."

An angry look crossed Lon's face. "I was afraid of that. She's been sinking her velvet claws into me every chance she gets. I suppose it's the schedule that's bothering her."

"You *are* almost a month behind."

"Don't you think I know that?" Lon shouted. Then his

voice dropped. "Sorry. It's just been one of those days —"

"What are the chances of catching up?"

"I'm working a full crew. I've hired additional men. I've pulled every possible string to get some needed material. I've hit every kind of snag you can imagine. Believe me, I'm doing the best I can!"

Cleve leaned back. He didn't doubt the man for a minute. He understood some of the obstacles Lon had been up against. The trouble was, Valerie didn't even try to understand them. The whole thing was some kind of playtoy with her.

"Come on out, Cleve," Lon said. "Let me show you a few things. You won't believe some of the bad luck I've had."

Lon tossed him a hard hat to wear and they left the trailer and stepped out into the September sun.

The building site was a beehive of activity. Russ Wagner's bulldozers were working, dredging out the earth for the pouring of foundations and pilings. Hammers echoed loudly and saws buzzed. Trucks hauling concrete were coming from Lewiston, rumbling down the road.

"You know, part of the trouble has been Miss DeReuss herself," Lon said with a frown. "She's made changes, and while they look like little things on the blueprints, they amount to days and long hours of work."

Cleve nodded.

"For instance, she decided she wanted the front entrance changed. We had to break out concrete, shore up other walls, pour cement again and send for a special stone from Colorado. This all takes valuable time —"

"That's exactly like women," Cleve said. "Especially when they stick their noses into a man's work."

Lon managed a short laugh. One of his men approached him, a blueprint in his hand.

"Got a minute, Lon?" he asked.

While Lon conferred with the man, Cleve looked around. He watched as a crane hoisted a steel beam into place. Another crane was unloading heavy wooden rafters from a flatbed truck.

There were men everywhere but Cleve noticed one in particular, probably because he wasn't wearing work clothes and somehow looked totally out of place here. He was drawing a bead on Lon. If everyone kept interrupting them, he never would hear all that Lon had to tell him.

As the man approached, he walked near the flatbed truck. As in a slow motion movie, Cleve saw everything in detail. The beams had jarred loose and were moving, rolling down from the top, and the man was directly beneath, in their path!

Cleve shouted. "Hey, look out! Hey —"

But his shout was drowned out by the roar of bulldozers and the man kept coming, unaware of the danger. Then, instinctively, he sensed something was wrong. He looked up and Cleve saw the fear on his face as he scrambled to get out of way in time.

"My God, he's been hit!" Cleve said. "One of those beams got him!"

They went running. The man had been knocked flat, with one arm pinned to the ground.

By now others had seen what had happened. All work stopped and the men came to crowd around.

"Get the beam off him!" Lon shouted. "Hurry up. And somebody call an ambulance. On the double!"

Cleve watched as the crane lifted the beam and moved

it away. Lon rolled the injured man over. He was out cold.

"Who is he?" Cleve asked.

"Don't know," Lon shook his head. "He's not one of my crew. Do any of you men know this guy?"

But none of them knew him or anything about him. Then Russ Wagner, who had been operating one of the bulldozers, stepped up, pushing his way through the crowd.

"That's the guy that asked me about getting a job," Russ said. "I sent him to your trailer, Lon. He must have been headed that way when —"

"What's keeping the ambulance?" Lon asked anxiously.

"There hasn't been time," Cleve said.

"All these months without one serious accident and now this happens. A total stranger. There will probably be hell to pay for this!" Lon said.

Cleve straightened. Valerie should be told about this.

"Could I borrow your phone, Lon?"

"Sure. Help yourself."

Cleve moved away, pushing through the crowd. Inside the trailer he tried to reach Valerie. But she had gone out and wasn't expected back until later in the day.

Cleve called Ed DeReuss's office next and finally was put through. He explained what had happened to Ed.

"I smell a fat lawsuit in the making," Ed said. "Listen, Cleve, do me a favor. Stay with this thing. I can't leave. I'm all tied up in an important meeting. Go to the hospital, get the man a good doctor — do what's necessary. I'll check with you later."

"But Ed —"

"No time to argue. Just do it."

Ed hung up. Cleve didn't want to get involved in the

business and he resented the way Ed assumed that he would drop everything else and look after his interests. But, for Valerie's sake, he would do what Ed had asked.

By the time he got back to the scene of the accident, he heard the ambulance coming. Russ Wagner was tramping about in his heavy boots, muttering to himself.

"My fault," he kept saying. "I should have warned him this was a restricted area, that no one was allowed in here without a hard hat. Now, he's been clonked on the head and it's my fault!"

"No need to borrow trouble, Russ," Cleve said.

"Easier said than done," Russ replied. "Seems like this is my month for trouble! You think he'll be all right, Cleve?"

"I'm going to get him a doctor. Ed DeReuss's orders. Stop worrying. He wasn't hit that hard."

But Cleve wasn't really as confident as he tried to sound. When the ambulance pulled away, siren howling and red light flashing, Cleve got in his car and followed.

He wasn't a bit happy about doing this but there was little choice. When he reached the hospital, he put the car in the parking lot and hurried inside. He'd try to reach Gretta. She was the best doctor he knew and he would trust her with the case. But first he would see what Emergency would tell him.

When he strode down the hall, he was relieved to see Gretta going about her afternoon rounds.

"Cleve! What are you doing here?" Gretta asked. "Visiting someone?"

"In a way. I was going to phone your office, but since you're here —"

"What is it, Cleve?"

"There's a man in Emergency. He was hurt out at the new clubhouse. I want you on the case."

"Is this official?"

"Yes. Ed DeReuss asked me to get the man a doctor. He wants the best. He's worried about a lawsuit. Can you, Gretta?"

"All right," Gretta nodded. "I'll see what I can find out. Wait here and I'll check with Emergency."

Cleve watched her hurry away, a small woman in a white doctor's coat who had a friendly word for everyone she met. She disappeared around the corner of the corridor. Cleve paced up and down the hall, waiting for her to return. When she came at last, she shook her head thoughtfully.

"I can't tell you much yet, Cleve. The man isn't badly injured. He's conscious now. But there's one strange thing."

Cleve eyed Gretta for a moment. She was saving the bad news till last.

"All right, let's hear it."

"The man can't remember anything."

"My God, you mean he has amnesia?"

"It's probably a temporary condition. We'll know more in twenty-four hours. There was a wallet in his pocket. His name is Tom Vogel and he's from New York."

Cleve absorbed this information for a moment. He'd have to report to Ed and tell him all he knew.

"Well, let's not borrow any more trouble than we already have, Cleve. Who knows, by tomorrow morning Tom Vogel's amnesia may be all cleared up and he'll be on his merry way."

Cleve smiled. "Always the optimist, aren't you? You

were always the one with the positive attitude. I can remember how you told everyone you'd be a doctor someday. And here you are. You love your work, don't you?"

"Yes, but sometimes it can frighten me too. This is my week for banged-up heads, it seems. First Sondra and now —"

"Sondra!"

"You didn't know?" Gretta watched him closely. "Russ Wagner ran into her, smashed up her rented car and left her with a bruised head. But she's doing fine. None the worse for wear by now."

"Thank God for that!"

"For someone who doesn't care, you seemed very worried there for a minute or two."

Cleve didn't reply but reached into his pocket for his pipe. He took his time filling it.

"How is she *really*, Gretta?" he asked.

"Fine."

"I want to know."

"I told you, fine."

"You know what I mean. You know her better than anyone. You've been close for years. I'm sure Sondra tells you things she wouldn't tell anyone else."

"And if she did, I wouldn't pass them on, Cleve. Not even to you."

He straightened in his chair and bit down on the stem of his pipe. "I never thought she'd go off the deep end like she did," Cleve said. "I knew she had a real hang-up about home and her ideas of what marriage is, but I never thought —"

"She was counting on you to understand how she felt."

"What was I supposed to do?" he asked angrily. "Some-

thing blew up in her face and she couldn't handle it. So, she took it out on me — on us — and she walked out —"

"You were pretty rough on her, weren't you?"

Cleve set his jaw. "I suppose, in all fairness, I'll admit we both said things we shouldn't have. It got out of hand."

"You underestimated her, Cleve. You underestimated her strength and her convictions and what she would do when pressed too hard. Even though she doesn't like to admit it, she's strong — like her mother."

"There's no point in discussing it, is there?" he asked finally.

"I suppose not. It happened. It's in the past. It belongs to yesterday."

"Yes," he nodded.

"Cleve —" She seemed about to say something. But then she changed her mind. "Nothing. It's none of my business. Forget it."

He was glad to leave the hospital. He drove back to the lake and found Lon Greene to tell him what little he knew.

"Amnesia! Brother. What next?"

"Gretta thinks it might not last too long. Think positively, Lon."

"I'll try. What did DeReuss have to say about all of this?"

"I expect you'll hear from him soon," Cleve said.

"Yeah," Lon sighed. "And how!"

Cleve started back to the city. But once again he found himself driving instead toward Wild Willow. The afternoon had dwindled away. The sky had a hazy afterglow of a late summer day and there was no spot he knew that

was any lovelier than Wild Willow at this time of day. He saw Sondra's car in the driveway. She was home.

Without letting himself think, he walked quickly to the door. Then he raised his fist and knocked.

10

ON MONDAY MORNING, Sondra had gone into Lewiston early. She had been at Carrie's house for just a few minutes when Maxine Davis arrived, toting a fistful of pencils and several large notebooks.

"Where would you like to start?" Maxine asked.

"Wherever you think best."

"Perhaps upstairs."

The upstairs hadn't been used in years, probably since Phillip had gone. Everything had been protected with dust covers. The rooms smelled stale. Sondra threw open the windows to the fresh September day and prayed for the strength to get this task behind her.

It was heartrending to say the least. But Maxine refused to let her get sentimental and they worked well together.

At lunch time, Maxine hurried away. Sondra was pleased with the progress they'd made. When the doorbell rang, she peered through the long, narrow window and found Gretta.

"Lunch," Gretta said, holding up two paper sacks. "From the fried chicken place."

"How sweet of you!"

"Ah, it's nice to come into this house again," Gretta said.

"Where shall we eat this?"

"The kitchen. I always liked Carrie's kitchen."

The chicken was crisp and tender. They ate hungrily, dividing the white and dark meat — Sondra eating the white, Gretta the dark — just as they had countless times before.

"How's your head?" Gretta asked.

"I'd nearly forgotten it. I still have a small bruise. I've tried to hide it by combing my hair a little differently."

"How's it going here?"

"We've barely made a dent. It's going to take forever!"

"Are you so anxious to finish?" Gretta asked.

"I do have a job in Los Angeles, you know, and my boss isn't the most patient man in the world."

Gretta frowned. "Then you intend to go back?"

Sondra wiped her fingers on a paper napkin and shook her head. "I don't know what I want to do. Everything's such a jumble. And I haven't told you what's really bugging me now."

Gretta cocked her small brown head like a bright bird and smiled. "Well, I'm waiting."

Sondra began explaining slowly, building up momentum as she went. The more she talked about the possibility of there being a grandson, the more convinced she became.

"What do you think, Gretta?"

"That you're whistling in the dark. If such a person exists, where is he? Why doesn't he come forward and why didn't he try to see Carrie all these years?"

"I've thought about that," Sondra admitted. "But Phil-

lip married a woman who wouldn't do Carrie any favors. By now, Tonya could be dead too, or remarried — who knows? The child may not even have known Carrie existed."

"Hon, why can't you just let sleeping dogs lie?"

Sondra folded her arms and leaned back in the chair. "I suppose it's all that money. I feel funny taking it. I have no right to it."

"Oh, you idiot!" Gretta sighed.

Sondra laughed. "Thanks."

"Well, you *are* an idiot! Carrie was a woman who did what she wanted. Besides, you earned the money. You took time to visit Carrie. You filled many an empty hour for her. That means a lot to older people."

"But it was fun —"

"You were really trying to take Phillip's place. Oh, don't look so surprised. That's exactly what you were doing. You took Carrie flowers on Mother's Day, brought little presents to her on her birthday and at Christmastime and God knows what else."

Sondra swallowed hard. "Now you're playing the psychiatrist."

"Call it what you will, but I think I'm right."

"I haven't wanted to ask and you've never told me," Sondra said, "but I know you were with Carrie when she died. Please, tell me about it."

"Carrie was not my patient. Dr. Baldwin had looked after her for years. But near the end, she asked to see me. I had visited her nearly every day, but this message reached me with a certain air of urgency. I think she knew —"

Gretta paused.

"What did she say to you?" Sondra asked.

"She asked me to find Phillip. Poor soul, she was confused. She'd forgotten her son was dead."

"There must have been so many times when she wanted him and he was not there!"

"There was one other person she asked for too, Sondra."

"Oh?"

"You," Gretta said gently. "You were the last —"

Sondra turned away. She left the table and went to lean against the window, trying to get a grip on herself. After a moment, she turned back to Gretta.

"Somehow, that makes me all the more determined to find her grandson. I'm going to *try*, Gretta. I have to do that."

After Gretta had gone, Maxine returned, and they spent a long afternoon working. Driving home, Sondra felt the tiredness and strain of the day. When she reached the house, she went out to the lake and strolled along the beach trying to relax. For a little while she sat on the dock, swinging her feet over the water, watching the boats. Mrs. Fulton was to have come today, but one look inside the cottage and Sondra knew she had not. She would have to phone her tomorrow.

Sondra had just gone inside and was thinking about fixing her supper when someone knocked at the door. Perhaps it was Mrs. Fulton at last.

In a dozen dreams she had opened the door to find him. A dozen times she had awakened with a start, heart pounding, for the dream never went any farther than that. Now he was standing there, very real, and this was no dream.

"Sondra?"

"What do you want, Cleve?"

"Now, that's not being very hospitable. Aren't you going to ask me in?"

He stepped past her and closed the door behind him, looking around with a curious expression on his face.

"It's just as I remembered. Carrie never changed a thing, did she?"

Cleve went to the fireplace and leaned against the mantle. He picked up a picture that Carrie had kept there. Sondra had intended to dispose of it but had forgotten to do so. It was a snapshot of Cleve and herself, arms entwined, laughing and happy. Carrie had always been fond of that particular photo.

"Happier days," Cleve murmured.

She found she couldn't say a word. Cleve put the photo back in place and turned to face her, his gray eyes watching her closely.

"Gretta told me you had an accident. I thought I'd stop by and see how you were."

"Your concern is very touching."

Cleve gave her a cold smile. "Is it necessary for you to be so biting?"

"The accident was nothing," she said more calmly. "That fool Russ Wagner ran into me, that's all. I got a bump on the head. But there's only a bruise left. The cut has healed."

"I'm glad to hear it," Cleve said. "You were luckier than the young man that got hurt at the new clubhouse this afternoon."

"What young man?"

"A stranger. Gretta tells me he has amnesia. His name is Tom Vogel. I was there when it happened."

"Will he be all right?"

"I think so. Given a little time. Time is supposed to be the great healer. Has it healed you, Sondra?"

The room seemed too small. She watched as he sat down on the couch in front of the fireplace and stretched out his long legs. He reached into his pocket for his pipe. As he filled and lighted it, he looked at her above the flame of his match.

"You didn't answer my question."

"I've made a new life for myself. I love Los Angeles. I have an interesting job."

Cleve nodded his head slightly. "Bully for you."

"Now who's being sarcastic?" she snapped.

"Would you like to continue this conversation over dinner at Antonio's?"

"No, thank you."

Cleve laughed. He leaned back and puffed at his pipe. "I dare you, Sondra."

"I don't care to indulge in childish games!"

"Oh, so that's what it is," he said.

"We said all there was to say to each other two years ago."

Cleve's face darkened. He clenched the pipe between his teeth.

"In two years' time, I had hoped you might have had second thoughts, that you might have faced the fact that you acted like some half-baked kid, that you irresponsibly went off the deep end."

Sondra's face felt hot. A vein was throbbing in her forehead.

"You didn't understand then, you don't understand now. You've got a blind spot, Cleve Ridgeway. Sometimes you can't see any farther than your nose. You can't feel

anything beyond current sensation. You can't comprehend how deeply others feel!"

Cleve got to his feet and began walking around the
room, looking at things as if he had never seen them
before. He was being maddeningly quiet, letting her
seethe in anger.

"What do you hear from your mother?" he asked.

She saw a curious light in his eyes.

"Very little."

"Are you going to tell me that you still haven't forgiven
her?" Cleve asked with a frown. "Two years and you still
hold it against her?"

"How can I forget what she did?"

"She did what countless other women have done in
countless other homes. She packed her bags and left. I
don't think that was such a crime."

"She destroyed Dad!"

"People fall out of love every day, Sondra," Cleve said.
"It happened to us, didn't it?"

"I don't want to talk about us!"

"What happened with your parents could be expected
to hurt young children, even teenagers. But you were
neither, Sondra. But you reacted as if you were. Such
immaturity!"

"Immaturity! It was my home. Shattered. I didn't know
why then, I don't know why now. They gave me vague
answers, vague reasons, but none of it made any real
sense. They were hiding something. They couldn't trust
me to understand. How did you expect me to feel?"

"I didn't expect you to go to pieces. I didn't expect you
to let it destroy us too!"

"Why did you come here, Cleve? Does it give you great

pleasure to drag me through all of this again? Did you come just to pick a fight?"

For a moment or two, the room was very quiet.

"I don't know why I came here," Cleve said at last. "But I know it was a mistake."

He stalked to the door and pulled it open. He turned back, and their gazes met and held for a stormy moment. Then he was gone, the door slamming shut behind him. The harsh ring of it echoed through the cottage and into her heart, a hopeless, final, destructive sound.

11

Sondra lay flat on her back, hands locked under her head, watching the play of shadow and starlight on the ceiling.

"I will close my eyes and go to sleep," she told herself. "I will not lie here another minute like this!"

She squeezed her eyes shut. She tried to think of peaceful things. Wind rippling water, the sound of a roaring mountain stream, or sand, soft and powdery underfoot. She thought of symphonies and high, sweet strings. She recited a favorite poem and she thought of the happiest day of her life. But that didn't work either, for that included Cleve and she was desperately trying to block him out of her thoughts and all the angry things they'd said to each other.

The next morning she was heavy-lidded and tired. For half a cent, she would take the first plane back to Los Angeles and let Quentin Hancock and Maxine Davis handle things here. Why did she feel so honor-bound to see to every little detail personally?

"Because of Carrie," she told herself. "Because I owe

her that much. Because I'm not going to let Cleve Ridgeway frighten me away!"

She had breakfast early. She was just pouring herself a second cup of coffee when someone knocked at her door.

"Who is it?"

"I'd like to speak with you, Ma'am."

She opened the door and found Russ Wagner. "I'm on my way to work at the clubhouse," he said. "I just wanted to stop by and see that you were feeling okay."

"I'm fine."

"I smell coffee," Russ said, sniffing the air. "Look, could you spare a cup? I haven't had any breakfast. I overslept."

Sondra hesitated, then nodded. "Come in."

He was wearing boots and clean work clothes. The familiar hard hat was in his hand. He tossed it into a chair.

"Say, this is a real nice place," he said.

She poured the coffee and handed him the cup.

"I see you got rid of the bandage on your forehead," he said. "Still sore at me?"

"Mr. Wagner —"

"Oh, call me Russ. Is the new car satisfactory? If it isn't, say the word and I'll get you another."

"The car will do nicely."

"Did you hear about the accident yesterday?"

Sondra said she had.

Russ shook his big head grimly. "That fella's got to be all right! He's just *got* to be!"

"Did you know him?"

Russ took a deep breath. "No. He asked me about a job. I sent him to talk to Lon Greene. I didn't warn him that he was in a restricted area, that a hard hat was required. If I had —"

"Accidents will happen, no matter what we do," Sondra said. "I'm living proof."

"But now that poor fella is lying in the hospital and doesn't even know his own name! Oh, his wallet said he's Tom Vogel, but that doesn't mean a thing to him."

"It's sad," Sondra said. Then with a wry smile, she added, "But maybe he's lucky in a way. He can start fresh, be a new man, whoever he wants to be."

Russ gave her a questioning look from his brown eyes and nodded. "I suppose. Still —"

He drank his coffee and put the cup on the kitchen table.

"I really stopped by to see if you'd like to go out to dinner tonight, Sondra."

He gave her an apologetic grin. "Maybe it would get me out of the doghouse with you."

"I suppose you were doing what you had to do on Wyler Street," she said.

"Yes, but somehow or other, you're blaming me. Seems like everything is getting all fouled up. Everything I do is wrong."

"Thanks for the invitation. But I think not. I've so much to do here."

Russ scowled and rumpled his curly hair with a big hand. "Yeah. I see."

He didn't believe her. He had seen through her excuse as if it were a pane of clear glass. He moved to the door, said good-bye and was gone, his boots ringing out noisily over the porch.

Sondra put Russ Wagner out of her mind and planned her day. The quicker she and Maxine could finish the work at the house, the better she'd like it.

They took turns writing the list, one calling off what to

put down, the other writing it. The list seemed endless. Every piece of silver, every dish, every knickknack, every stick of furniture — every single item in the house had to be cataloged.

She was glad when it was time to close the house and go back to Wild Willow. How many more days like this could she endure? It was unseasonably warm and the skies were an incredible blue. In L.A. she often didn't see the blue of the sky for days due to the smog. This was a true luxury.

Mrs. Fulton had cleaned the cottage. Sondra was relieved to see this the minute she walked inside. From the window she eyed the lake. The water looked enticingly warm. She used to leave a swimsuit here at Wild Willow.

"I wonder if I can find it," she murmured aloud.

It took a few minutes of searching. Then she changed quickly, snatched up a towel and left the cottage to run down the wooden dock and pause at the end of the landing. The water looked as deep and inviting as ever. Without another thought, she dived in. The water came rushing over her head. She touched bottom and surfaced. She began to swim, finding it a kind of joyous release to pit her strength against the water, to give all her thought to the task of moving swiftly, surely.

She swam until she began to feel tired. Then she turned back to the shore and waded out onto a small stretch of sandy beach. The sun was warm and the sand powdery beneath her feet. Spreading her towel, she stretched out. She listened to the songs the sand sang, echoing now and then with the roar of a motorboat, the shouts of a skier, and over it all was the lazy lap of water against the shore, soothing her, easing her.

"So, here you are!"

She opened her eyes to find Gretta.

"Hi," Sondra said. "Join me. There's another suit in the cottage."

"Maybe another time. I have to make rounds at the hospital in a little while. How's the head?"

"It's all right. Stop worrying about it."

"Well, this is one of my wounded heads that has turned out all right. I wish the other one would."

"You mean the man that was hurt at the clubhouse? How is he?"

"Physically, he's fine. But he still can't remember anything. He knows he's Tom Vogel because of the papers in his wallet. He has a New York address. But that's *all* he knows."

"What's he going to do?"

"I'm sure I don't know. Perhaps go back to New York and see what he can learn about himself, although I don't advise that just yet. I think he'd be much better off to stay here for a few days. This amnesia business may clear up quite suddenly and unexpectedly."

"Will you stay for supper?" Sondra asked.

Gretta laughed. "I was hoping you'd ask. If you make it early — I still have those rounds to make."

"I'll take one more dip to wash off the sand and I'll be ready to go in. It cools off so quickly this time of year."

Sondra spent only a brief moment or two in the water, then waded out and wrapped herself in the towel Gretta held for her. Together they walked back to the cottage.

"I had two reasons for stopping by," Gretta said. "I've a favor I'd like to ask."

"Ask away."

"Tom Vogel is going to be released from the hospital, probably tomorrow. He has almost no money. But he does

have a key to a room at the Grandview, so apparently he was staying there. He'll need work. I want it to be something light to start with, something he could work at as he pleases. You mentioned needing someone to help with your yard."

"Goodness, yes! It's a mess."

"Would you consider Tom?"

"Why don't you send him around and I'll talk with him."

"Well and good! You're an angel, Sondra!"

"Do you give all your patients such royal treatment, fixing them up with jobs and everything?"

"No. But I feel sorry for Tom. He's a likable chap."

"Does he interest you?"

"Only as a patient," Gretta replied.

"When are you going to make some man very happy by marrying him?"

"Probably never."

"You have so much to offer!"

"What?" Gretta asked. "Aspirins for a headache? Remedies for the flu? All kinds of free medical advice?"

"Why don't you be serious?"

"I'll leave the romance department to you, Sondra."

Inside the cottage they started preparing their evening meal. The phone rang.

"Ten to one that's for me," Gretta said. "I gave my answering service this number."

Gretta took the call. She spoke briefly and hung up.

"I have to go. Sorry."

"Who's going to eat all this food —"

But Gretta had already darted out the door. In a moment, Sondra heard the sound of the car driving away.

She thought momentarily of inviting Lon Greene to eat

Gretta's share of the supper but quickly discarded the idea.

It was just a few minutes later that someone knocked. She went to answer the door, hoping that for some reason Gretta had come back.

"Hi, sweetheart."

"Dave! Dave Manning!"

He stepped into the room and put his arms around her to lift her from the floor and swing her around and around, laughing.

"Let me look at you, Sondra. Ah, that's my girl."

"Oh, Dave, it's so good to see you!"

"Hey, what's the matter?"

She dabbed at her eyes. "Nothing. Just happy you came, that's all."

"Give old Uncle Dave a kiss."

He gave her a hug and she dropped her head to his shoulder. Dave Manning had been her father's best friend, a man who had been in and out of their lives at odd times, popping up whenever he was in Lewiston.

"How long will you be here this time? Oh, I hope it isn't just a hello and good-bye!"

"Not a chance this time, honey. You won't believe it, but I finally took that desk job. I'm in Lewiston to stay!"

12

"You don't mean it!" Sondra laughed. "I never thought you'd come to it."

Dave reached up to loosen his bright tie, then shed his jacket and tossed it to a chair.

"I'm getting tired of the road, hotel rooms and bad restaurant food . . . Say, have you had dinner?"

She smiled and shook her head. "No. And you're in luck. Gretta was here but got called away. You can have her share."

"Great! Are you as good a cook as your mother?"

"Probably not," she said.

"No one could cook like Helen," Dave said. "I suppose that's why I used to make a beeline for your house whenever I hit town. It wasn't just your dad's company, it was your mother's cooking!"

"And you were always so welcome," Sondra said wistfully. "Oh, Dave, everything's changed so!"

Dave nodded. "Yes, it has. Your dad's dead, your mother's left town — I know everything sort of went to pieces for you a couple of years back."

"And now Carrie!"

"I heard about that. Imagine, my little girl, an heiress!"

"I still don't believe it."

Dave did just as he had always done at their house. He took off his necktie and loosened his collar. He sat down at the table with a sigh.

"Looks wonderful, Sondra. I'm hungry. I had a long drive getting here today."

"Don't be bashful. Wade in and eat."

Dave laughed and did just that. It seemed so good to have him across the table from her. It was almost as if nothing had changed. But Dave looked older. There were new, deep lines in his face, his hair was silvery gray, and she noticed a stoop to his slender shoulders.

When they had reached the final cup of coffee, Dave leaned back in his chair and lighted a cigarette.

"Let's talk," he said. "Tell me what's been happening."

"You already know. Dave, did you ever know anything about Phillip Winterhall?"

"Carrie's son? Sure. A little. He was about my age. But we never moved in the same circles. There was always a lot of talk about him."

"Do you remember when he married a woman named Tonya?"

"Matter of fact, I do. Why all the questions?"

"Please, just answer, then I'll explain. Okay? Did Phillip and Tonya have any children? A son?"

Dave looked thoughtful for a moment and tapped his cigarette into the ashtray. "Not that I ever heard of. But I sort of lost track of Phillip after he left and got married. He went abroad, didn't he? Or east. Something."

"And you don't know anything more?"

"No," Dave shook his head. "What is it, pet? What's bothering you?"

Slowly, carefully, she explained. Dave lifted his brows.

"I get the feeling you're wanting to make some kind of noble gesture if there is a grandson."

"Perhaps. Is that wrong?"

Dave reached out and held her hand for a moment. "Most people would take the money and run. But you never were like anyone else. You were apart from the crowd."

"Dave, how do I find out if there is a grandson? What do I do? Quentin Hancock is plainly not going to help me. He thinks I'm full of nonsense."

"Let me think about it for a minute," Dave said. "In the meanwhile, if there's any more of that good coffee —"

She filled his cup. He picked it up and carried it to the couch in front of the fireplace.

"You know, as a cook, you run a close second to your mother. By the way, you haven't told me about her."

"Nothing to tell," she said quickly.

"You hear from her, don't you?"

"Occasionally."

"I take it things aren't going too well between you."

"No."

"Who's fault is that?"

Sondra looked up with an angry flash of her eyes. "I suppose you think it's mine!"

"Easy, honey. You're putting words in my mouth. But I've been around in this old world long enough to know that there are always two sides to everything."

"You were Dad's best friend. Didn't he ever confide in you? Didn't he ever tell you what went wrong?"

"He said it would no longer work with Helen. They were making each other too unhappy. I think this had been going on much longer than you knew, Sondra.

Maybe as far back as when you were a youngster in school."

"Are you telling me that they stayed together for my sake?"

"It's done everyday, sweetheart," Dave said. "But who can really pinpoint why a marriage goes sour?" Then he laughed. "Look at me, a confirmed bachelor, giving out marital advice!"

"How did you escape marriage, Dave? All these years on the road, you must have met dozens of women."

"Sure. I met them. But I was never in one place long enough to make it count. Besides, there was someone. A woman who wasn't free."

Sondra stared at him, wondering if he was teasing, but she saw that he wasn't and she was shocked.

"I never knew that!"

Dave nodded seriously. "It's true, nonetheless. Let's get back to your mother. I want you to patch it up with her, Sondra."

"She's the one that left," Sondra pointed out. "Not me. Why should I go running after her?"

"Spoken like a twelve-year-old child!" Dave chided. "Come off it, Sondra. You're a grown woman. Time to take life in your stride. Time to forgive and forget."

He made it sound so simple. But it wasn't. She only knew that when Mother left, everything began to go haywire for her. All her ideals and concepts of home and what it was suddenly disintegrated right before her eyes. It warped her thinking, she knew. It made her cautious and leery of love and marriage. Because of Mother she had run scared, and in turn that had led to breaking off with Cleve.

"I see I haven't even made a dent," Dave said.

"I can be as stubborn as Dad was," she replied.

"And he lived to regret it," Dave pointed out.

"I'm quite aware that after Mother left and Dad lived only one year longer, his life was not a happy one. But *he* was not to blame."

Dave shook his head. "It's pointless to talk to you, Sondra. You've got a one-track mind. Now, let's get back to the matter of Carrie's grandson. I've got an idea. It ought to be a simple matter to check this out. But it would take a professional. Once there was a detective agency in town. Is it still there?"

"As far as I know."

"I used to know one of the girls that worked there. Diane Edgar. Give her a call. If there's anything to be learned about whether or not a grandson exists, Diane can find out for you."

"Would it be expensive?"

"Probably," Dave nodded. "But you've got the money."

She laughed. "Yes. I keep forgetting that. You know, Uncle Dave, I think I'll do that!"

"Anything to keep you happy," he smiled. "I hope this settles it in your mind for once and for all. Now that that's cleared up, is there any chance I can have a second dessert?"

"Bad for the waistline."

"Honey, at my age, who cares?"

They talked far into the night and it was late when Dave said he must be going.

"We both have busy days tomorrow," Dave said.

"Where are you staying?"

"At the Hotel Lewiston for now. I'll take a small apartment. One of the girls at the office has promised to help me find one. I'll see you again soon, Sondra."

Dave kissed her cheek and for a moment she hugged him.

"It's so nice to have you home, Dave. It's a little like having Dad."

"That was the nicest thing anybody ever said to me. Good-night, honey. Keep in touch."

She stood in the doorway and watched him go, waving to him. It was time for him to be settling down. Pounding the highways as a salesman for an automotive supply house had never been easy. But she wondered if he would truly be happy working behind a desk.

"What can I do for you, Miss Tracy?" Diane Edgar asked the next morning.

When Sondra explained, Diane didn't blink an eye. Probably such matters were routine in a detective's office. She took notes and leaned back in her chair.

"I don't have much to go on. You're positive that Phillip and Tonya were married in Philadelphia? You're sure of the date?"

"Yes. I have a newspaper clipping to that effect."

"Then our logical place to start is Philadelphia," Diane said. "I'll fly there and see what I can find. Often, these cases lead us to several places. You understand this, don't you?"

"I want the grandson found, no matter what the cost," Sondra said.

Diane nodded. "I'll do my best. I'll report to you as soon as I've found any concrete information."

Sondra was relieved to have put the wheels in motion. Dave's suggestion had been a good one. Diane Edgar could put an end to all the questions she had.

The work at Carrie's house seemed to be slowing down.

Or perhaps it was just her own restlessness that made it seem so. Maxine was very thorough and careful. She seemed to be a capable woman, married and a grandmother, who had picked up her old job to fill the suddenly empty hours after her son married. She talked a great deal about her son and small granddaughter.

"I ramble, don't I?" Maxine laughed. "I try hard not to be one of these doting grandmothers, but I don't seem to succeed too well."

Sondra had trouble keeping her thoughts in a straight line. She loved Carrie's house. She loved all the furnishings. How could she sell them? But on the other hand, how could she take them all back to Los Angeles? That was a bridge she would have to cross soon. Perhaps when Diane Edgar came back from Philadelphia with her report, it would be easier.

When she drove to Wild Willow that evening, she slowed down as she neared the construction site of the new clubhouse. She saw Lon Greene and he motioned for her to stop. He came to lean against the car and peer through the open window at her.

"Hi! I've been calling Wild Willow all afternoon."

"I've been out all day."

"It's going to be a perfect evening. How would you like to go out to dinner? It won't be Antonio's this time. I have a better idea. A surprise. Say you'll come."

Lon's sunburned face was handsome and appealing. So totally different from Cleve's. Perhaps that was why she liked him so much.

"All right."

"Good. I'll be by about seven or so."

She had no sooner reached home than she heard a car in the drive and looked out to see Gretta. There was a tall

young man with her, dark of hair and quick of eyes. He looked to be about her own age, possibly a year or two younger.

"This is Tom Vogel," Gretta said. "I promised to give him a lift to the Grandview Hotel and thought we could stop in on the way there."

Tom seemed pleasant and likable. He looked about the yard and nodded. "Yes, I could work here," he said. "I could spruce it up until it looked real nice."

"I need a good hand," Sondra said.

"I'd do my best, Miss Tracy," Tom said anxiously. "Things are a little bewildering to me yet, but I know I can do this. Don't ask me how I know, but I do!"

"Consider yourself hired. Can I expect you in the morning?"

"I'll be here."

"You'll find lawn tools in that little shed over there. If you need anything more, let me know."

Tom Vogel nodded almost happily. "Thank you, Miss Tracy. Thank you a lot!"

He shook her hand and seemed boyishly eager to please.

When they had gone, Sondra forgot about Tom Vogel and looked ahead to her evening with Lon Greene and began to sort through her clothes for something to wear.

The phone rang. She wasn't really surprised to hear it was long distance calling. In a moment, Harry's gruff voice was on the other end of the line.

"Sondra, when are you coming back to Los Angeles?" he asked.

"I can't give you a truthful answer. Things here get more involved every day."

"I need you."

"I know, Harry, and I'm sorry. But there is just so much to be done."

Harry muttered to himself and, after a few minutes' persuasion, agreed to give her more time.

"Wind it up in the next couple of weeks, will you?" he asked.

"I'll try. Harry, I'm just as anxious to come back as you are to have me. How're things in the shop?"

"Busy. I handled most of the orders you were to get in Rome and London by phone. We'll have to hope for the best."

"You're a dear, Harry."

"Among other things!" he said gruffly. "Now, hurry back."

Then Harry said good-bye and hung up. But hearing his voice again had reminded Sondra that she had responsibilities there too.

As she dressed for the evening, she tried to put it all out of her mind. She wanted to relax and have a nice time and she knew Lon would be good company.

Lon was a little late and apologetic about it when he came.

They drove around the lake to Pete Shaffer's place. Pete rented boats of all types. He waved to them when he saw them.

"Everything's ready and waiting, Mr. Greene."

"Thanks, Pete. Come along, Sondra."

"We're going for a boat ride?" she asked.

"We sure are," Lon smiled. "This way."

The boat was actually a small cabin cruiser, one of the nicest that Pete had to rent. Lon gave her a hand aboard and then took the wheel, Pete helping him ease out from

the dock. In a moment, they were speeding over the water, leaving a wide foaming wake behind them.

Lon flashed her a smile. "I wish I owned a boat like this."

"It's very nice and you handle it like a pro."

"My family used to vacation at a lake resort when I was a kid. I learned a lot about boats."

They skimmed the water faster and faster and there was exhilaration about the mere fact of speed. He turned and cut a wide circle, looking for the quietest place in the lake. He finally settled for the exact middle, cut the motor and let them drift for a few minutes. Then he dropped the anchor and turned to her.

"We'll go below," he said. "If Antonio has done everything I asked, we'll have a superb supper."

"Antonio?"

"Catering is not something he normally does, but when he heard it was for you — well, it seems you're one of Antonio's favorites."

Sondra laughed. "That was sweet of him."

"It's all supposed to be here," Lon said.

They went down the steps to the quarters below. Lon peered into the refrigerator and nodded.

"Good, good!"

The oven in the small stove was on and Sondra opened the door. The heavenly smell of spices and mushrooms came out to her.

Lon pulled plates and glasses from the tiny cupboard. Together they made the small table ready and Sondra took the hot dishes from the oven. Lon opened the bottle of red wine, poured a glass for each of them and lifted it to her.

"A toast," he said. "To an evening we'll always re-member."

"You'd spoil a girl, Lon."

"That's my intention."

Lon turned on the radio to some music and they ate hungrily, laughing over their appetites.

"It must be the night air."

"Combined with Antonio's good food," Sondra said. "This was a nice idea, Lon."

There was a hot fruit compote simmering in brandy for dessert. Lon carried it to the upper deck and they ate it there, watching the stars begin to come out. They could see all the lights of cottages around the lake, and yet they seemed very remote from everyone else, very much alone.

"You know," Lon said thoughtfully, his voice reaching her through the twilight, "when Valerie DeReuss decided to build a new recreational area here, I wasn't sure it was the right location."

"You must remember this is September. The summer crowds have gone."

"I know. I've been here since spring and I was sur-prised at how busy the lake was. The hotel was full nearly every week."

"The cult today is to get away from it all. So everyone goes rushing to the mountains and lakes and what do they find when they get there? People. Traffic. Noise. The very thing they wanted to escape."

"Not quite," Lon disagreed. "It *is* different. Careful, lady, you're knocking my trade."

"Oops. Didn't think about that."

Lon laughed. He came to take the cup from her hand and set it aside.

"Let's move over to the railing. We'll catch more breeze there."

When they leaned against the railing, he put his arm around her shoulders.

"When I came to Lewiston and Reynolds Lake, I thought it was going to be just another job, Sondra. Now I don't think that at all."

She was aware of the warmth in his voice. Slowly, he turned her to face him. The boat rocked gently. The stars were out and from the running light on the bow, she could see his face, the curly blond hair, the smile on his firm lips.

He bent his head. She stood perfectly still. His kiss came down on her lips, quick and warm. She wanted to respond. She wanted to cling to him, to give him back his kiss moment by moment, but it didn't work.

He let her go at last.

"I want to see more of you, Sondra. And I will."

13

THE NEXT MORNING Sondra was awakened by the telephone. She knew instantly that she had overslept. Shaking the sleep out of her eyes, she went to answer it. She gripped the phone tightly with a sharp intake of breath. She had not expected to hear Cleve's voice. Their last angry encounter was much too fresh in her mind.

"Don't hang up on me!" he said quickly. "I'll get right to the point. I'd like to see you. Let's have dinner tonight."

"Dinner?"

"I've got a business proposition to make."

"What possible business could we have?"

"Shall I call for you at the cottage or would you rather meet me at Antonio's?"

"Cleve, why are you doing this? If you simply want to continue the fight, forget it. I've had all of that I want."

He took a moment to reply. She knew he was carefully controlling the tone of his voice. "I told you, this is business. College business and not my idea at all. If there was any other way to handle it, I would. But this happens to fall in my department —"

"What have I to do with college business?"

"If you don't want to have dinner alone with me, then bring Gretta. But, please, be at Antonio's by seven this evening."

He hung up and she held the dead receiver for a moment. Then she slammed it down. The gall of the man!

She was still angry when she reached Carrie's house. Maxine quickly tuned in to her mood and they worked almost silently throughout the morning. All through a hasty lunch and a busy afternoon, Sondra vowed that she would not keep the appointment with Cleve.

But when she reached Wild Willow that evening, she walked out to the dock and stared across to Antonio's. Why had he chosen to meet her there? Was it a deliberate test, another one of his games? Did he want to twist her heart with painful memories and then sit back and gloat?

Well! There was a way to handle that. She'd go! She would show him that Antonio's meant nothing. It was just another place to have a nice dinner. She would be as cool and indifferent as she could possibly be. "I'm going to open your eyes tonight, Cleve Ridgeway!" she thought.

With that determination she scrubbed under the shower, rubbing her fair skin pink. She spent several minutes brushing her hair until it crackled and shone like spun gold. She looked at herself for a long moment in the mirror. Had she changed in these last two years?

"A few new little lines around my eyes," she thought. "Laugh lines."

Or were they really scowl lines? It didn't seem she laughed much anymore. Her skin was still smooth, her brows finely shaped and the color of ripened wheat, her

nose a duplicate of her mother's. But her mouth was different. Full, gentle, perhaps a bit sensuous. The mouth didn't belong to either Mother or Dad. She wondered what long and forgotten ancestor had given that to her, as well as the tiny little dimple that appeared unexpectedly at the corner of her mouth when she smiled or laughed. There was something almost devilish about that dimple.

She was deliberately late reaching Antonio's. She walked inside, head up, a coolness about her that anyone could sense. Cleve was in the lobby, waiting.

She was struck by how attractive he was, from the black, thick hair to the gray eyes. He watched her calmly as she crossed the lobby to him. They were like two strangers. Good! It was the way she wanted it.

"I've told Antonio you'd be along shortly. I think he has a table ready for us," he said.

Antonio came to greet them. He was beaming happily, clutching the shiny menus under his arm.

"What a sight! The two of you together again. Like old times, eh, Cleve?"

Cleve's face colored. Sondra clutched her purse tightly.

"Come along," Antonio said. "Everything's ready."

Sondra saw at once that Antonio was taking them to their old table. He pulled out the chair for Sondra with a delighted air.

"I knew this was a red letter day when I got up this morning," Antonio said. "My horoscope said so!"

"Horoscope?" Cleve laughed. "Why, Antonio, I didn't know you believed in such things."

"The stars rule our lives," Antonio said. "How can anyone doubt that? Why do you think God put them up there?"

Antonio bustled about, making certain everything was

just right. With a snap of his finger, he summoned a waiter who came with a red towel over his arm to fill the water goblets, ice tinkling. Then he held a match to a candle and withdrew to give them time to study the menu. All this while, Antonio hovered nearby, watching intently. Then he gave them another beaming smile and nodded his head happily.

"Enjoy your dinner. I'll send your favorite wine. Compliments of the house. For old times' sake," Antonio said with a wink.

Then at last they were left alone with the sputter of the candle and then night falling softly on the lake.

"I know what you're thinking," Cleve said. "And I did *not* plan it this way. It was all Antonio's idea."

"What's it matter?"

Cleve's dark brows arched up for a moment. He began to study the menu intently. They decided what they wanted and ordered. Sondra noticed that Cleve did not order his favorite dish. Nor did she.

"How are things going at Carrie's house?" he asked.

"Slow," she replied.

"It must be rough on you."

She was surprised by the gentleness of his voice.

"Yes," she said.

"I understand Maxine Davis is helping you."

Sondra nodded. "She's been a godsend."

"Maxine's very capable. She did some work for us at the college once. You should visit our old Alma Mater someday, Sondra. There have been changes. One new building, a new wing to the old science hall —"

Sondra remembered the campus. Sharp, minute images. Ancient trees, winding walks, vine-covered buildings, classrooms smelling of chalk and textbooks, the

library with its rows and rows of books, sunlight through storm-splattered windows, footsteps in the hall, muffled laughter, a kiss in the rain.

She pulled her thoughts away. She would not think about that. But it was almost as if Cleve had remembered the same thing. Across the table, his eyes were flickering and he toyed with the folded linen napkin, pleating it nervously.

"Carrie loved the college," Cleve said. "Did you know she donated to it regularly? In memory of Phillip."

"No."

"I'm curious. Why did she forget us at the end?"

"I don't know. Is that why you wanted to see me? Do you want me to make a donation to Lewiston College?"

Cleve gave her a smile. "No. I'm not here to solicit funds, but it does have to do with the college and with Carrie, at least indirectly."

She was puzzled. Cleve leaned his elbow on the table, chin cupped in his hand and he seemed relaxed, calm.

"It can wait, Sondra, until after we've eaten. Pleasure first, then business."

He gave her a long look. She tore her gaze away. It was a trick of the candlelight, a witchery cast by Antonio's horoscope's red letter day, but it would be so easy to forget the past two ragged years, to pretend nothing had ever happened between them.

"Sondra, do you remember the hurricane lamp that Carrie had. It was on the spinet. It was old, ornate and very beautiful."

"Yes. It's still there."

Cleve smiled. "I always liked that lamp. She told me once she'd give it to me to remember her by."

"I remember."

"Would you consider selling it to me, Sondra?"

She shook her head. "No."

"All right. As you say."

"But I'll give it to you. Just as Carrie would have wanted me to do."

"Thank you," Cleve said. "I'll stop by the house someday and pick it up. If that's all right . . ."

The waiter was back. They ate their salads and Cleve talked about professors they had known, old friends in Lewiston and the changes coming in the town. He touched briefly on the new freeway, and when she seemed sad, he turned to other topics.

He was very pleasant, almost informal. She was surprised and relieved. She was not up to doing battle with him again. But she wished the evening were over, the business, whatever it was, settled.

Antonio had done himself proud. The food was superb and Cleve smiled. "He's put his best foot forward. It's like him."

When they had reached the final course, Cleve got down to business.

"I don't mean to be presumptuous," he said, "but I've heard you plan to sell Carrie's house. I want to buy it."

She stared at him. "You? Why on earth —"

"Not me. The college. I'm here as spokesman for it."

"I don't understand."

"One of the fraternity houses has been inadequate for many years. They've wanted something larger for a long time. Carrie's house is huge and would serve very well. It's not too far from the campus and I'm sure —"

"You have to be out of your mind! You want to turn

Carrie's house into a fraternity house! Fill it with noisy, clumsy, reckless boys? The place would be ruined, spoiled —"

Cleve took a deep breath and leaned back. "If you sell it, what does it matter what happens to it?"

"It would matter a great deal to me!"

After a moment, he shook his head. "I should have known. You're still all tied up with *things*."

"You were an idiot to have asked in the first place!"

"Then accept my apologies," he said. "Do you intend to live in the house yourself?"

"I'll be going back to L.A. as quickly as I can."

"I see."

Antonio came bustling toward them.

"How was the food, my friends?"

"Great," Cleve nodded. "Very nice. Very special."

Antonio put his fingertips to his lips and blew a kiss. "Only the best for you. Now, listen, I have a surprise —"

He signaled the small orchestra that had been playing quietly all evening. In a moment, the music changed and with a start Sondra looked up to find Cleve's burning gaze watching her closely. It was their song! How had Antonio remembered that?

"For you!" Antonio said. "Go ahead, dance! Remember you two are champions."

"That was for the Charleston," Cleve pointed out carefully.

"Nothing like a nice, romantic song," Antonio said. "Now go on . . ."

Cleve got to his feet and held out his hand to Sondra. "Let's not disappoint the man," he said.

There was nothing Sondra could do without making a

scene. Cleve's fingers closed around hers and he led her out to the floor. Stiffly, she went into his arms. He held her loosely, as if afraid to touch her.

"He's watching," Cleve said with a tight smile. "He's got some crazy idea about getting us back together again."

"Crazy," she repeated.

He pulled her a little closer. His chin brushed her forehead. They moved uneasily around the floor, but Cleve was as good as he had always been. It was almost fun to follow his familiar lead, to let the music direct their steps.

The background began to fade away. The tables were just soft splotches in the dim room, dotted with candle flames and beyond the window, the sky had turned deep with autumn. The trumpet soared and the trombone throbbed. The music unwound Sondra's nerves and released a flood of memories. Yesterday was gone. It was only now, this minute, this second, that counted. Nothing else.

Cleve looked down at her. His gray eyes were warm.

"Hello, little girl."

He used to call her that in the tenderest of moments. The music went on and on. She dropped her head for only a moment to Cleve's shoulder. Then it seemed too difficult to lift her head, to push away from him. His arms were close around her and none of it seemed real. It was one of those hazy dreams that she so often had, that awakened her with a pounding heart.

Then the song ended. For a moment, Cleve still held her close and he buried his face against her hair.

"Let me go," she said.

"Antonio's watching."

"Let me go!"

He laughed softly and released her. She walked ahead of him to the table. There, she snatched up her purse.

"I must go."

"The evening is young!"

She didn't listen. She walked out of the room, cheeks stinging.

"Sondra —" he called after her.

But she didn't stop. She didn't listen. She ran to her car and drove away as quickly as she could.

"Fool!" she told herself. "Why did you let any of it happen?"

14

THE EVENING with Cleve had left Sondra in a strange mood. She tried hard to be angry. She kept telling herself it had been some kind of scheme, one of his games, and then another more sensible voice told her that was nonsense. Cleve's attitude had been warm, friendly. He had seemed anxious to please. She remembered his face against her hair, the feel of his arms around her, and then everything bad she had thought about him became a lie. When she had run out of Antonio's, had she been running from him or herself?

Working with Maxine Davis the next morning, Sondra found it hard to concentrate. The work made her edgy, although Maxine was as enthusiastic about it as ever.

"My word!" Maxine exclaimed. "Look at this Dresden china. It's a design I'm not familiar with. I'm sure it's very old and very rare. If you're interested in selling it, I know a collector who would be wild to have it."

"I haven't decided to sell anything," Sondra said sharply. "If you can work alone this afternoon, I've a few other things to do."

"Of course!"

She had no other plans, but it seemed she suddenly had to escape the house. Things were beginning to crowd in on her.

She would go home to Wild Willow. There, perhaps, she could find some measure of peace, some direction to follow. As she drove out of the city, she found herself turning in the opposite direction, and soon she had reached DeReuss Park. She had not been here for a long time, not since she had left Lewiston in a cloud of despair, determined to mend her life elsewhere.

The rich greenness of the grounds and huge trees never failed to soothe her. She drove into the cool tunnels made by entwining branches overhead and found herself going to one particular place. It was her favorite.

Bittersweet Garden overlooked the lazy Mississippi River. It was a place of cool stone walks, bright flowers, hidden benches and whispering leaves. A small fountain splashed and a statue stood in mute solitude guarding the bluff, a memorial to yesterday. A bandstand stood lonely in the sunlight but echoed with whispers of music, stamping feet and laughing children.

There was a stillness here broken only by the chattering of a gray squirrel, the faraway sound of a train and an echo of memories.

The first time Cleve told her he loved her, they had been here. Every other important occasion had been climaxed here — birthdays, graduation, and a ring he gave her to bind her to him forever. They thought of Bittersweet Garden as their own private little world.

But, as lovely as it was, she wished she hadn't come today. Why think back? What good did it do? It was gone, like Indian smoke on the hill, like rain to the ocean, like blossoms to dust.

She walked away quickly and drove to Wild Willow. She would not dwell on Bittersweet Garden, or Cleve, or on those perilous moments last night when she had almost let down her defenses and reached back to yesterday.

At the cottage, she made straight for her swimsuit. She spent a vigorous half hour in the water before she waded out and stretched in the sun. The lake had been cooler today and the sun had lost some of its strength.

She watched a cloud go scudding across the sky and her memory began playing tricks on her again. She saw Cleve's face bending over hers, water dripping from his black hair.

"Hello, mermaid," he had said that day not really so long ago. "My lovely mermaid!"

"And if I'm a mermaid, who are you?"

"I'm your captor. I'm going to carry you away home and keep you forever."

"It will never work. Come sundown, I turn back into a fish."

Cleve had bent down then and kissed her with fierce ardor.

"Sundown will never come," he murmured. "I won't let it. But just in case it does, I'd better not waste a moment . . ."

She remembered how he kept kissing her until she scrambled to her feet to escape him and went running and laughing into the water. He splashed after her, caught her by the ankles and pulled her under. There in the green water of Reynolds Lake he had kissed her again.

They were lazy, sunlit days of summer, moments stolen whenever they could, coming to Wild Willow because they both loved it here and because Carrie had given them the run of the place. Sometimes Carrie had been

there too, sitting on the porch, watching, smiling and calling to them.

But of all the times they had been here, she remembered best the days of autumn. She loved the colors of the turning trees, the haze of Indian summer, the sound of locusts and the smell of burning leaves. Autumn had its own fragrance and soon that essence would be here again. September was nearly gone and October would come riding in on blue skies and bright sunlight, bringing a nip to the night air, brushing color to the apples, orange to the bittersweet, red to the sumac and gold to the maples. Those cool October evenings would mean a fire in the fireplace and Wild Willow would grow more snug with each passing day.

She turned her thoughts away. She would not be here that long. She would be back in Los Angeles. Somehow she had to make a plan to leave here, to get her affairs in order. She wondered anxiously what Diane Edgar was finding out in Philadelphia.

Sunday, Sondra invited Gretta to spend the day with her.

"We'll have a lazy time," Sondra promised. "I think you could use a day like that."

Sunday bloomed perfectly. Sondra prepared a picnic lunch and they feasted on the beach.

It was early in the afternoon when Tom Vogel stopped by. He had made a good start with the lawn and Sondra was pleased to see Wild Willow beginning to look neat and trim again. Tom had a few questions about his work and Sondra told him all he wanted to know.

"How are you, Tom?" Gretta asked.

"Feel fine, Dr. Berglund. But I still can't remember a

thing. I wrote some letters to New York. I found a name and address in my wallet. I don't know who Mrs. Brown is, but I wrote to her anyway. Maybe I'll learn something that way."

"Remember my advice. Go slowly," Gretta said.

Tom looked out to the lake for a moment. "Say, did they ever find that fishing boat that sank out there? Did they ever dredge the lake and bring it up?"

Sondra and Gretta exchanged surprised glances. When the boat had sunk it had been the talk of everyone around the lake. But it had happened nearly fifteen years ago!

"What boat was that, Tom?" Gretta asked carefully.

"I don't know. A fishing boat. One Pete owned, wasn't it?"

"Tom, where did you hear about the boat?" Gretta asked.

Tom shrugged his shoulders. "I don't know. Doesn't everybody know —" he broke off and turned about. "Hey! How did I know about that? Did a boat *really* sink out there?"

Gretta nodded. "Yes. You're sure no one told you about it since you've been here?"

"I-I don't know," Tom said, his face clouding. "Maybe that's the way it was. Maybe I didn't really remember anything after all!"

"And again, maybe you did," Gretta said. "This may be the beginning, Tom! It may happen very slowly. Maybe next week you'll remember something else, maybe even tomorrow —"

Tom gave a tired sigh. "I sure do hope so! I know I'm Tom Vogel — but I could be anybody and feel just as funny about it."

Tom left a few minutes later, looking thoughtful and unhappy.

"You really think Tom's on the brink of regaining his memory?" Sondra asked Gretta.

"We can't ignore the possibility. For his sake, I hope so."

"But if he's from New York, why would he be remembering something about the lake?"

"Good question," Gretta said. "Perhaps Tom lived here once or knew the vicinity."

They heard the sound of a car horn and looked up. In a moment Russ Wagner appeared on the dock.

"I thought I saw you down there."

"What brings you out this way?" Sondra asked.

"Why the pretty girls, what else? Matter of fact, I've come to take you to dinner." Then he swept a glance in Gretta's direction. "Both of you."

"I'm sorry," Sondra said. "I already have a date."

Russ frowned. "Oh. Well, Gretta —"

Gretta sifted the sand through her fingers and shook her head. It was plain that Gretta had been an afterthought. She was a sensitive woman and Sondra knew that she would refuse Russ now, no matter what.

"I have to make rounds at the hospital this evening."

Russ didn't say anything more. Sondra saw a boat skimming across the lake in their direction and soon she recognized Lon at the helm. He waved to them and eased the boat up to the dock. In a moment, he had tied up and joined them.

"Hello, people. How about a ride?"

"Good idea," Russ nodded.

"Sounds like fun," Gretta said.

Lon reached a hand to Sondra. He was wearing swim-

ming trunks and his muscular body was brown with the sun. "Nothing like starting our evening early," he said.

Lon helped her aboard. In a few moments, they were on their way. Sondra turned her face to the breeze and let her hair fly. Lon gave her an appreciative glance.

When he had phoned early that morning for a date, her first instinct had been to say no. Then she quickly changed her mind. How better to get Cleve out of her mind and her heart than to find someone new?

The boat was fun. Lon cut a few circles and figure eights that made Gretta clutch the side of the boat and Russ laugh. Russ began to tell them what were supposed to be funny stories. No one laughed but Gretta.

"Sorry, guess I'm not the best storyteller around," Russ said with a sigh."

"I thought it was cute," Gretta said.

"You're just being nice, lady," Russ murmured.

"How did you get in the heavy equipment business?" Gretta asked.

Russ shrugged. "It was a family thing. My uncle owned the outfit originally. He wanted to retire. I'd been working for him even when I was still in school, and I knew it could be a good business. So, when he offered to let me buy it, I took him up on it."

"You really enjoy running those big machines?"

"You can bet your boots on it!"

"Yes," Sondra spoke up quickly. "He loves wrecking people's houses."

Russ flushed. "I've told you, Sondra, that was business and out of my control. I don't have anything to say about where the freeway goes. I just do some of the work."

"When will it be completed?" Gretta asked.

"Another two years."

"Two years!" Gretta said. "That long?"

"You've got no idea what it takes to make a road like that."

"It's rather a fascinating business," Gretta replied. "And you're working at the new clubhouse too."

"I've only got three machines there. All that's needed though."

"And things aren't going fast enough," Lon spoke up with a frown. "I'm still getting all kinds of static from the front office."

"You mean from Valerie?" Sondra asked.

"Not directly, but indirectly," Lon said. "It would be a mistake to underestimate her."

"Yes." Sondra nodded.

She remembered how Valerie had been with Cleve, clinging to his arm, making it plain to everyone that he belonged to her.

"How's Tom Vogel doing, Gretta?" Russ asked.

"As well as can be expected."

Russ frowned. "You know, he's kind of a funny guy. I took him out to supper. I tried to talk to him and help him a little. I got the feeling he didn't appreciate it."

"You must remember he's going through a traumatic experience, Russ."

"Yes, but — well never mind. It's the same old story. Every time I try to do something for somebody, I get my foot in it. For example, I saw Vogel in Lewiston the other evening. He ignored me. I know he saw me. But he just went right on — he acted like he was, well, I don't know. Forget it. It's just one of my crazy ideas, but he seemed sort of sneaky."

Gretta laughed. "Your imagination is working overtime."

Lon slowed the boat and Sondra saw that they were nearing Pete Shaffer's place. After they docked, Lon and Russ disappeared toward the soft drink machines.

"I'd better check with my answering service," Gretta said. "I'll use Pete's phone."

Gretta came back smiling, so Sondra knew there were no immediate problems. Gretta had gotten a little sunburn on the tip of her nose. With her brown hair windblown, she looked relaxed and happy. The day had been good for her, and Sondra was slowly beginning to realize something else. Gretta liked Russ. She supposed he was nice enough. She knew it was crazy to blame him for what had happened to her house on Wyler Street, but the sight of it had gripped her with such despair that she had childishly sought someone to put the blame on and Russ had been it.

Russ was not the man she would have chosen for Gretta, but still —

Gretta chatted with Pete Shaffer for a while, and when Lon went for a can of gas for the boat, Russ sat down beside Sondra on the pier.

"Look, how about dinner tomorrow night?" he asked.

Russ was being persistent and Sondra didn't want to seem unfriendly or impersonal, but she shook her head.

"Thank you just the same, Russ."

He took a deep breath. "I sure do bat zero with you, don't I?"

Gretta came back to join them and she looked thoughtful.

"I was asking Pete if Tom Vogel had been around talking to him, asking questions. But he hasn't. I thought Pete might have told Tom about the boat that sank in the

lake. But that wasn't the case. I think Tom really has remembered something!"

They cruised around the lake a little while longer Then Lon suggested to Sondra that she change clothes when they dropped Russ and Gretta back at her dock.

"We might as well take a drive before dinner," Lon said. "You can come back to the hotel with me and I'll change, then we'll be on our way."

"All right," Sondra said.

Lon dropped an arm around her shoulder and she didn't move. He was nice. Attractive. Interesting. She would have as much fun tonight with him as she could. She would not once permit herself to think of Cleve or the dinner she'd had with him at Antonio's. She would live for this hour, this moment.

15

L ON DROPPED Russ and Gretta at the Wild Willow dock.

Russ was not exactly pleased to find himself alone with Dr. Berglund. He'd come to Wild Willow with the sole idea of taking Sondra to dinner. She was such a pretty girl, with that silky blond hair and those blue eyes. There was strength to her, too, everything from the way she walked to the lift of her chin and the set of her shoulders. Russ admired strength in a woman. God knows, they got the brunt end of things. Raising kids, keeping house, making their way in a man's world. It wasn't easy. He'd watched his mother do it alone for many years after his father died. But somehow she'd managed to keep them together, the whole parcel of them, until they were big enough to be pushed out of the nest.

The heat of the afternoon had begun to dwindle. Gretta went to gather her beach things. Russ helped her fold her huge towel and they had to find her sunglasses, which had been partially buried in the sand. Gretta was no raving beauty, but she had a nice little build and her smile was so warm it lighted up her whole face.

"Listen, why don't we have dinner? Couldn't you make rounds at the hospital first and then go?"

She eyed him.

"I just thought," Russ said in a flustered voice, "you're alone, I'm alone, and we have to eat — why not together?"

"Well, all right. If you don't mind waiting while I make rounds."

They drove to the hospital, not talking very much.

She invited him inside. "You can wait in the lobby if you want."

He sat uncomfortably in one of the chairs. For a while he played the people-watching game. Then he began pacing around. What was taking so long? Then he spied Gretta at the desk, in a white doctor's coat, giving instructions. She flashed him a smile and waved, disappearing again.

It was nearly half an hour before she returned.

"Finished," she said.

"How're all the patients?"

"All doing fine. No one on the critical list or in intensive care right now, so I think I'll enjoy my dinner very much."

He felt like a giant walking beside her. Sometimes his size was a liability as well as an asset.

He held the door of his car for her and she slid in. Then, with a roar, he started the motor and they drove away.

"Why did you want to be a doctor?" he asked curiously.

"It was my childhood dream," she answered. "And a few times I didn't think I'd make it."

"You mean all that studying —"

"I had no problems with that," she said. "It was a

matter of finances. My family simply couldn't help very much and it was mostly up to me."

"I see. I understand about that. Dad died young and never left us a nickel. It was only my uncle who had anything and that was the fleet of bulldozers. Of course, the way equipment costs these days, that was quite a lot."

"And now you've acquired them. So you've made some big strides yourself."

Russ grinned. He had to say one thing for her, she was good for a man's ego.

"I'm still up to my eyes in debt," he laughed. "But I'll make it. One of these days I'll be free and clear."

"I'm sure you will."

"Have you seen the progress of the freeway lately?"

"I catch a glimpse now and then when I drive to the hospital."

Impulsively he decided to take her down to the construction site. Building a freeway was no simple job, and while he did only a part of the work, he was proud of what he and his men had done.

"Hope you won't mind a rough ride down to the bottom," Russ laughed.

He moved a barricade and drove down the road the cement trucks had been using. It was rough and pitted but Gretta seemed game as he drove straight to the trailer he used. It served as his office, and from here he supervised all the work and occasionally left it to run one of the machines himself. The paper work was a necessary thorn in his side, something that had to be done. But he liked climbing up on the big machines, starting them up and putting them through their paces, watching the earth move as he directed it.

His machines were lined up beside the trailer, like huge soldiers waiting to be sent to the front for duty.

"It looks different from down here," Gretta said. "It will certainly change the appearance of Lewiston."

"Yes," he nodded. "And think how it will handle the traffic."

"Still, I hate to see the changes," Gretta said.

"You and Sondra!" he sighed. "But let's face it, we can't hold back progress. If it hadn't gone through here, it would have been some other part of the city. This was the logical site. It connects with the bridge over the Mississippi." He began explaining how they had done the work, how many man hours and machine hours had been put to use since they had started.

"We had all those summer rains which didn't help, but we're about on schedule again. I've got a good crew. They're loyal. They know how much it will cost me if we're penalized for being late getting the work done."

"I'm impressed," Gretta said.

He laughed, pleased. "You know, I have a feeling you really understand all of this."

"I'm trying," she said with a smile.

"Let's find some dinner. I've bragged about my work long enough."

But it was nice to find a woman who at least tried to comprehend what he did here and what pride he took in his work.

The Crossroads was crowded and they had to wait. He should have phoned ahead. But Gretta didn't seem to mind. At last they had a table and they ordered. Russ liked the way she gave him her full attention. He found himself talking about his mother and his six brothers and

sisters. Before he knew it, he had told her practically his
entire life story.

"You don't play fair," he grinned. "You've been making
me do all the talking."

She laughed. "I wanted to hear."

"What about you?"

"You'd find it dull. My life has been medical books for
so long — studying, working . . ."

"How did you manage it?"

"I don't even like to remember. They were such hard
years. I was within sight of my goal when I thought I'd
have to drop out. This is something I've never told anyone
before. Carrie Winterhall financed me my last year at
medical school. I'm proud to say I had paid back every
penny before she died."

"This Carrie must have been quite a gal."

"To say the least," Gretta nodded.

"But why did she leave everything to Sondra? A friend,
not even a relative?"

"Carrie had no one else. She did things because she
wanted to do them."

Russ studied her for a moment. "And so do you, don't
you?"

She laughed and her plain face was suddenly pretty.

"I'll confess. Yes, I do."

"You're a good egg, Gretta. A real good egg."

There was a kind of resigned wistfulness about her as
she smiled at him.

Somehow he felt he had insulted her and he didn't
know why. When they had finished their meal, he
politely suggested a drive or a movie. But she refused and
he saw her home.

He found himself driving out toward the lake again. He left his car near the clubhouse site and got out. As he always did, he went to check his machines. Only three of them were here, but they represented a large investment and he liked to keep an eye on them.

It was dark, but as Russ approached the machines, he thought he saw someone slipping away stealthily. He frowned. Something was going on! Once he'd had trouble with young fellows stealing gasoline.

"Hey!" Russ shouted. "Who goes there?"

The shadow moved again, this time at a dead run. Russ shouted again and went after him. He had not been a football tackle for nothing, and as he gained on the slight figure he lunged forward, grabbed for his legs and brought him down. There was a grunt as the man hit the ground.

Russ scrambled to his feet and hauled him up by the collar.

"Okay, what were you doing snooping around my machines?"

"Russ, it's me. Tom."

Russ stared at the young man in the deepening darkness and saw that it was indeed Tom Vogel.

"The question still goes, what were you doing here?"

"Let me go and I'll explain," Tom said. "I know it must sound silly, but I thought if I came over here and looked around, maybe something would jog my memory."

Russ let him go. He was doubtful for a moment, but remembered what Gretta had said. The poor guy was having a bad time of it.

"I guess that makes sense. I hope I didn't hurt you when I tackled you."

"Surprised me would be better."

"Why did you run?"

Tom lifted his shoulders in a shrug. "I don't know. I guess you just gave me a scare and my nerves are a little ragged."

"You were coming from the west. Had you been somewhere else?"

"Just walking around the lake. That's all. It's a free country, isn't it?"

Russ laughed. "Sure. Sorry."

"It didn't work anyway," Tom said. "You won't have to worry, I won't be back anymore."

"Let's go and have a drink somewhere."

"I'd like to, Russ, but I don't think I'll take you up on it this time. I'm sort of wrung out —"

"Yeah, I can see how you would be."

Tom seemed anxious to be on his way. Russ let him go and watched him walk hurriedly toward the hotel. Russ frowned. Tom's story had sounded right. Then why was it he didn't believe it?

Russ decided he might as well go too. When he walked back to the car, he found someone else just arriving. In a moment, he saw Valerie DeReuss getting out of her car. He called to her.

Valerie turned with a start. "Oh, it's you, Russ. What are you doing here?"

"Looking things over, same as you."

"You didn't finish those footings for the south wing, did you?"

"No. But we've made a good start."

"The excavation was to be completed two weeks ago, the footings in by the end of this last week!" Valerie said angrily. "What's taking so long?"

"Ma'am, Lon's working his men as hard and fast as he

can. But you know how it is. Materials don't arrive, things go haywire — it's the name of the game, Miss DeReuss."

Valerie lighted a cigarette, and in the flame, he saw her beautiful face, the silky hair and cool, green eyes. She was not a woman to be taken lightly. For that matter, her father, Ed DeReuss, was a VIP around Lewiston. Everyone knew he ruled things with a hard hand. But somehow Valerie didn't fit into the business picture.

"This was a great idea," Russ said. "But how come you took it on, Miss DeReuss?"

She laughed shortly. "To show people I can do a few things more than just play bridge, buy fancy clothes and drive jazzy cars. Good enough?"

Russ lifted a brow. "I see."

"Dad didn't think I could do it. Nor did Cleve. Well, they were both wrong, weren't they?"

Russ nodded. "Yes, Ma'am, they were."

"And stop calling me 'Ma'am.' It makes me feel a hundred years old."

"Sorry."

"Valerie will do just fine," she said. "How would you like to buy me a drink? The bar at the hotel is still open."

Russ was taken by surprise. They hardly moved in the same circles, but he nodded. "Sure. Why not?"

They decided to walk to the Grandview. Russ could smell Valerie's expensive perfume and her voice through the darkness was cool and nice to hear. Russ was sure every eye in the place was staring at them as they entered the bar.

They talked about the clubhouse and touched briefly on Tom Vogel. Then Russ got an earful, all directed abusively at Lon Greene. He didn't envy Lon, for it was

clear Valerie intended to raise Cain with him again tomorrow.

"Why are you by yourself tonight? Where's Cleve Ridgeway?" he asked.

Valerie crushed her cigarette out with a vicious motion. "Cleve had other plans. I think he went to see his father. They're close."

Russ laughed. "And you don't like the idea?"

"I didn't say that."

"You didn't have to."

"Let's just say that Cleve's father and I didn't exactly hit it off the one and only time we met."

"I see."

"But it doesn't matter," Valerie said. "I'm going to marry Cleve and I don't care who doesn't like it "

"Have you known each other a long time?"

Valerie sipped her drink. "We were in college together. Even in the same crowd. Only then — well, Cleve had other things on his mind."

"You mean, other girls?"

Valerie stared at him. "Yes. One in particular. But I don't care to discuss her."

"What's he do at the college, exactly?"

"Financial Coordinator."

"Fancy title. Is it a fancy job?"

"No," Valerie said. "Not equal to his ability. But that will change one of these days soon. I want him right over there at the clubhouse as manager. Dad's agreed."

"That leaves Cleve," Russ said pointedly.

Valerie nodded. "Yes. But he'll come around. He'll see it our way."

Russ knew that Valerie would probably give Cleve no

peace. She had her head set, her velvet claws out. She gave Russ a sweet smile that was totally deceptive.

"You will push a little harder tomorrow and get the ground ready for the footings, won't you?"

"I'll be finished before noon. After that — Lon's your baby, Valerie."

Russ walked her back to the car. She put a hand on his arm and smiled at him.

"Thanks, Russ. Don't let me down tomorrow."

Then she blew him a kiss and was gone.

16

Sondra had just returned to Wild Willow when her mother arrived by taxi. Helen Tracy was still attractive, with wisps of gray mixed in her brown hair. She had gray eyes with warm lights and a figure that defied her middle-aged years.

"Aren't you even going to say hello, Sondra?"

Sondra drew a ragged breath. They had not seen each other since Mr. Tracy died.

"Hello, Mother. How did you find me here?"

"I heard about Carrie. I wanted to be here for the services but I couldn't. I knew you'd come."

"You've heard about the inheritance?"

Helen nodded. "Yes. Cleve told me."

"Cleve!"

"I've taken a room at the hotel. We ran into each other in the lobby. He told me I could find you here."

She stepped into Wild Willow and looked about her for a few moments. "I'd forgotten how snug it is here," she said. She dropped her purse into a chair and moved to the window to look out to the lake. "Sondra, I've come back for a very specific reason."

"I was sure you had," Sondra said coolly.

Helen turned about to look at her, her face compassionate.

"Sondra, I know things have been wrong between us for a long time now."

"Two years to be exact!" Sondra said. "The day you left Dad —"

Helen bit her lip. "I want you to forgive me for hurting you so. I didn't intend that. I want you to believe that more than anything on this earth!"

"Asking forgiveness now comes a little late."

"I tried to ask it before I left, but you wouldn't listen," Helen pointed out.

Sondra knew that this was true. She had shut out her mother, coldly, deliberately. Because from the beginning, she had sided with her father.

"I never understood then and I can't understand now why you did what you did," Sondra said.

Helen sighed. "I know. And there are certain things I don't want to discuss with you. They were very private and personal matters between your father and me. I did what I thought was best for all of us."

"You simply wanted to be free!"

"Yes. I wanted to be free. Because I could no longer live with your father. But I don't want to discuss that either. I only want to erase this bitterness between us, this anger."

Sondra watched her mother as she clasped her hands together and looked at her with anxiety in her eyes.

"It's too late for that," Sondra said.

"I don't believe it is ever too late," Helen said. "That's why I've come back. I'm going to relocate here. Find a new job and pick up the pieces the best I can."

"I thought you intended to marry your boss, Ross Howard."

Helen shook her head. "That's all off. It didn't work out . . . Isn't there someone at the door, Sondra?"

Sondra had been so preoccupied that she hadn't heard the car stop in front of the cottage.

"Dave!"

It was David Manning.

"Am I interrupting something —" Dave asked. Then he caught sight of Helen Tracy. "Helen, is it really you!"

"Dave!" Helen said with a happy smile. She reached out both hands to him and Dave took them tightly in his own. Then Dave hugged her and kissed her cheek.

"You're a sight for sore eyes, Helen. How are you? Why are you here?"

"It's a long story," Helen said.

"And I want to hear it all. Listen, I came by with the intention of taking Sondra out to dinner. Now, we'll all go."

"I-I don't believe I care to go, Uncle Dave," Sondra said. "But if you and Mother want to go —"

Dave looked from one to the other. Her mother's cheeks were flushed and Dave gave Sondra a lingering glance.

"I'd love to go, Dave," Helen said. "If you'll excuse me, I'll freshen up."

Dave gave Sondra a knowing look. "You're acting like a child, Sondra."

"Am I?"

"You know you are," Dave said. "And I won't tolerate it. Your mother's home where she belongs. You're here. I'm here. I want us all to go out together, and by George, we're going!"

"It won't work, Dave," Sondra shook her head. "There is just too much wrong between us —"

"Then we'll straighten it out. And we're going to start by going to dinner," Dave said firmly. "Listen, your mother's made the first move. The least you can do is make the second!"

"You're shouting, Dave," Sondra said.

"You're darned right, I am. I'll shout some more if necessary."

"All right, all right!" Sondra replied. "I'll go. But I'm not going to enjoy one minute of it!"

Dave reached out to take her by the shoulders. He shook her gently. "That's my girl. And get the chip off your shoulder. Relax. You might find out things aren't half as bad as you think. Go put on your prettiest dress. I'm going out with two lovely women tonight and I intend to show off both of them!"

The restaurant was in the west end of Lewiston and called the Chalet. Dave knew the headwaiter and they were given one of the best tables.

Their waitress was not as young as some there, and had at one time probably been a beauty. Now her graying hair was rather drab and her cheeks were sunken.

"What's good tonight?" Dave asked her.

The waitress gave him a dim smile. "The special. Or the filet mignon."

After considerable debate they decided, and the waitress went away. Helen frowned. "She looks familiar. Someone I should know. I guess not, though."

"It doesn't take long to forget people," Dave said. "It can happen in even two years' time. I'm just glad you're back to stay, Helen. Tell me what I can do to help."

"First, I'll need a place to stay. A small apartment will do."

"Persuade Sondra to stay in Lewiston and move into Carrie's house with her," Dave said. "Heaven knows, it's big enough for both of you."

Helen's glance came across the table to Sondra.

"I'm sure that would never work."

"I'll not be staying," Sondra said quickly. "I'll be going back to L.A. soon."

"But I thought —" her mother's voice trailed off.

Dave changed the subject and began to talk about old times. He and Helen discussed mutual friends, Mr. Tracy, Dave's work and what Helen had been doing while she was away. Sondra felt left out of things, even though Dave tried to draw her into the conversation from time to time. They were still talking when their food came.

After what seemed a very long time to Sondra, they left the Chalet. Dave suggested they drive to Wyler Street and see the changes the freeway had brought. It was the last thing Sondra wanted to do. But Dave was insistent and Helen was curious.

"You won't know it," Dave said. "Your old house is gone, Helen."

"I heard it would be taken."

Sondra watched the familiar landmarks going by her window as Dave turned down the north end of Wyler and drove south down the wide street. The trees were huge here. They drove by Carrie's house and Sondra flicked a glance in its direction. She had come to love that place even more since she had come back. But she must not think of such things. It didn't really belong to her. It belonged to Carrie's missing grandson.

Then Dave was stopping the car at the barricade blocking the street.

"Oh, dear! I had no idea it would look like this!" Helen said.

"It gives a person a start," Dave said, as they got out.

Sondra couldn't endure it. She turned away, eyes wet. Would it always tear her heart to come here, to remember?

She went back to the car. In a few moments, Dave and her mother returned. They drove away silently.

Dave planned to take them back to Wild Willow, but Sondra didn't want to talk with her mother anymore tonight. She couldn't.

"Dave, would you mind dropping me off at Gretta's apartment?" Sondra asked.

"Of course not."

She was glad he didn't argue. He drove straight there and she was relieved to see a light burning. Gretta was home.

Gretta was slow in answering the bell. "Sondra! Where have you been? I've been trying to phone."

Sondra explained.

"So, your mother's back," Gretta said with surprise "You weren't expecting her, were you?"

"Heavens, no!"

"How did it go?"

"About the way you'd expect. What are you doing?"

Gretta had newspapers spread on her kitchen table, where she'd been filling three small flowerpots with soil. "Transplanting some of my plants. I'm not doing something right. One of them is dying."

Sondra smiled. "If it's not humans, it's plants. Don't you ever tire of taking care of sick things?"

"No," Gretta laughed. "I don't!"

The phone rang and Gretta put down her trowel. When she came back to the kitchen, Gretta gave Sondra an apologetic smile.

"It's an emergency. Maxine Davis's granddaughter."

"Debbie? Maxine worships that child!"

"I know."

"What's the problem?"

"I'm not certain but it sounds serious. How will you get home, Sondra? I'm sorry, but I won't have time to drive you."

"Don't worry about it. I'll call someone. Run along, Doctor, don't keep your little patient waiting."

Gretta snatched up her doctor's bag and with a wave of her hand was gone. Sondra looked up the number of the Grandview Hotel and called Tom Vogel. In a moment, she heard Tom's voice on the other end of the line. She explained her predicament and Tom promised to be there within a few minutes. Then Sondra went outside to wait, enjoying the autumn evening with its touch of crispness, the smell of falling leaves.

"You're sweet to come for me, Tom."

Tom gave her a nod. "No bother. I enjoyed the drive. It's a great night."

They left the city and were soon driving down the lake road. They were nearly home when, abruptly, Tom put on the brakes.

"What's wrong?" Sondra asked with alarm.

Tom stopped the motor and gripped the wheel tightly.

"It's the strangest thing, Miss Tracy," he said. "All of a sudden, I remember another time I was driving along a lake. One a lot like this one. When I was a kid. A long time ago —"

"Think hard, Tom," Sondra said. "Try to remember. Who was with you? Where were you?"

Tom laughed shortly. "I don't know. It came to me in just a flash. I think I was with my mother. I don't mind telling you, Miss Tracy, this is driving me right up a wall! Every once in a while, I'm almost on the edge of remembering something and then it's gone —"

They drove on at last and Tom pulled into her driveway. "Well, as old Ben used to say, what you have to wait for the longest is the best when you get it."

"Old Ben? Who is that?"

Tom turned to her with a startled look on his face. "By golly, I don't know, Miss Tracy. Somehow the name just popped out — like remembering driving along a lake."

"Ben Hacksman?" she asked. "Tom, would it have been Ben Hacksman?"

Tom rubbed his forehead with an anxious hand. "I don't know. Maybe. Does that mean something?"

"I'm not sure."

She decided not to tell him that Ben Hacksman had lived here on Reynolds Lake, that every young person who ever came here had known him. Ben was always saying that what you had to wait for the longest was the best when you got it, especially when the fishing was poor. Could the lake Tom remembered be this very one? Is that why he had come here? Because the lake was familiar, a part of his background? But if that were true, why didn't someone recognize him?

She opened the car door. "I'm sure you'll straighten it all out in your mind soon, Tom. Good-night. Thanks for coming to drive me home."

He nodded to her and she hurried away to unlock the

front door. She heard the phone ringing inside and
dashed to answer it.

"Miss Tracy?"

"Yes."

"Diane Edgar."

17

"I'M STILL in Philadelphia, Miss Tracy."

"I see. Does that mean things have not gone well?"

"Slow. Very slow. But I'm getting it, bit by bit. I want facts, records, written reports, newspaper items, things that are trustworthy."

"But you know now that there is a grandson, don't you?" Sondra asked.

"I haven't said that at all, Miss Tracy. I hope to be home by the end of the week. I'll be in touch then."

Sondra was disappointed that Diane Edgar had not found something more concrete to report. Or was she holding back until she came home?

Sondra was suddenly very tired. She thought of Carrie's huge house on Wyler Street and what it contained, the work left to be done there. She kept remembering her visit with Nona Campbell, the feeling that Nona had lied, that she *did* know about a grandson. If Diane Edgar unearthed him, what right did she have to any of Carrie's things?

"A legal right!" Quentin Hancock would argue.

But what about the moral right? The human right?

Money and property were one thing. But they weren't everything. She loved Wild Willow. Perhaps she could manage to keep it — still, why should she? She must return to Los Angeles as quickly as possible. Now, with her mother here, a constant reminder of all that had happened, it would be easier to go.

Yes, quickly, very quickly, she must make plans to leave Lewiston for good.

Gladys Shaw left her job at the Chalet at midnight. Her feet hurt. She hated the job as a waitress but it was best under the circumstances. Who looked twice at a waitress? Once in a while, when men like Dave Manning came in, they were generous with the tips and the job looked a little better. But all of this was necessary so she'd just do her best to get along and bide her time.

The Chalet was in the far end of town and there was no bus service this late at night. It meant riding an expensive cab to the rooming house where she was staying. She kept telling herself that things would get better soon. They had to! This time, she wasn't going to give up. This time the big dream was going to come true.

The rooming house was in a poorer part of town, but it suited her purposes just fine. Everybody kept to themselves. No one paid any attention to who came and went. It was what she wanted, to be a faceless woman, a nameless soul, just another roomer who didn't rate a second look or thought.

The only thing good about the Chalet was the fact that they served great meals and she had befriended the cook. At closing time he always gave her a sack full of food. Sometimes it was sandwiches filled with thick ham, sometimes steak. There were pastries too and occasionally a

half bottle of wine. Going home, she would feast at one o'clock in the morning and sometimes Sonny joined her. She was expecting him tonight. He had phoned her at the Chalet to tell her he'd be by.

The cab dropped her at the rooming house. She went inside the dingy, dimly lighted hall and climbed the stairs to her room. The apartment was all in one room with a hot plate and a sink for a kitchen, a couch that made into a bed at night, and a tiny bath. But it would do for now. She could endure this and wait for things to get better.

The door was unlocked. She pushed it open cautiously.

"Hi," Sonny said.

"So, you're here already," Gladys said.

"What's in the sack."

"Food," Gladys smiled. "Hungry?"

"Always hungry," Sonny laughed. "How's it going at the Chalet?"

"About like you'd expect. How's it going with you?"

Sonny grinned. "Great. Just great. It's going to work. I know it is."

"It *has* to work," Gladys pointed out. "We can't afford any mistakes, Sonny."

Sonny's face darkened. "You have to think about that?"

"A police record is a police record, no matter how you look at it. We're on file, dearie, and don't you ever forget it."

Sonny shook his head. "I'll *always* remember that. Let's eat. . . . How were the tips?"

"Most of them were fair."

Sonny patted her shoulder. "Don't you worry. It won't be long until things will be better. I promise you that."

"You really think we're going to pull this off?"

"Why not?" Sonny shrugged. "We've pulled off lots of cute little tricks. Don't see why this one won't work."

"Still . . . I don't know. This is a *big* caper, Sonny."

Sonny laughed and reached into the paper sack to see what he could find, while Gladys kicked off her shoes and rubbed her aching toes. Soon they sat down at the table and ate. Sonny began to talk about all the things they'd do when they were rich.

"Won't be nothing too good for us," Sonny grinned. "We'll go places, do things. We'll even sail on a ship across the sea. We'll really live it up!"

Gladys nodded. "Sure, we will. *If* — "

"Now, don't talk like that!" Sonny scolded. "It's going to work, I tell you. I know it is."

"I wouldn't be too sure."

They ate in silence for a while, thinking about their plans, talking about them in detail, double-checking everything. It sounded good. It *could* work. Sonny was sure it *would*. But Gladys had been around a lot longer than he, and she knew that plans often went astray. She was a walking example of that. What had ever worked out right for her? The answer was simple — *nothing!*

They finished off the last of the contents of the paper sack and Sonny wadded it up and tossed it into a waste-basket.

"I'd better get back," he said. "Drop by the hotel tomorrow like I told you."

"You think I ought to do that?"

Sonny grinned. "Yeah, I do. It will work in just fine if you're seen coming there. Okay?"

"I hope you know what you're doing."

Sonny walked to the door. "See you around."

"Be careful!" she called after him.

But he hadn't heard her and it wouldn't matter if he had. He was fired with determination. She could only hope that it would go as well as he expected, without a hitch. But sometimes she couldn't believe that it would — but she was willing to take the chance.

"I'd like to be lucky just once in my life," Gladys said aloud.

It was the first time since she'd come to Lewiston that she had kept anything back from Sonny. But she hadn't been able to tell him. In the first place, she wasn't real sure. But she was fairly certain she knew the woman she'd seen at the Chalet dining room. She hadn't changed much over the years.

"Not like me," Gladys thought. "I haven't had the niceties of life like her!"

She convinced herself that it was just as well she hadn't told Sonny about it. Sonny would get nervous — no, that wasn't right. *She* was the nervous one. Sonny had enough grit for them both. She'd have to rely on that. But God knows she'd be glad when it was all over, when they were in the clear.

18

CLEVE RIDGEWAY usually had breakfast in the hotel's coffee shop. This morning as he went down he spied Sondra's mother. When she had checked into the hotel, he had spoken with her briefly. Now he found that he wanted to continue the conversation. He walked over to her table. "Mind if I join you?"

"Of course not. I'd like your company. I never liked eating alone."

Helen was still a pretty woman.

"Did you see Sondra?" he asked.

Helen nodded. "Yes. Yesterday. Last night Dave Manning took us both out to dinner."

He knew how much Helen had looked forward to seeing Sondra again, but he knew too that she was hesitant and worried about the encounter.

"How did it go?" Cleve asked. "Or should I ask?"

"Yes. You may ask. It went as I expected. Sondra was cool and polite, but not very friendly, and I know she'd rather I hadn't come."

There was a sadness in Helen's voice that touched him.

"I'm sorry. Sondra can be stubborn."

"Yes. She can," Helen nodded. "But I'm not going to give up, Cleve. I *won't* give up. I know I've made my share of mistakes in the past, but I want a second chance. Do you think she'll give it to me?"

Cleve frowned and reached in his pocket for his pipe. He took his time filling it, thinking about Sondra. She was a strong-willed girl. She always had been. Even when they'd been in school together, she had not been one that bent easily.

"If she decides she wants to give you the second chance, she will," Cleve said. "Once she sets her mind, that's it. For both your sakes, I hope she decides to be reasonable. I think you did the right thing in coming back, Helen."

Helen smiled. "Thank you, Cleve. You always were a young man after my own heart."

Cleve laughed at that. "I know. And I was glad. But I was never as sure about Sondra's father."

"Arnold was always too possessive of Sondra. They had a special rapport between them. One that even I couldn't break through. I suppose that's one of the reasons Sondra took it so hard when Arnold and I separated. I'm to blame for what happened between you two, aren't I?"

Cleve tapped the stem of his pipe against his teeth.

"I wouldn't say it was your fault. But it rocked Sondra to the core. It did something to her. It was the first really big blow that she'd had to take and she found she couldn't handle it. So she ran away — from me, Lewiston, everything."

"But she's back now. Do you think she'll stay?"

"No."

Helen Tracy lowered her head with a sigh. "She's so proud, so terribly foolish — if only I could tell her . . ."

"Tell her what?"

Helen shook her head quickly. "Nothing."

"What are your plans, Helen?"

"I've decided to stay here. Lewiston is home, after all. I liked the East and I had a good job there, but there were problems. It seemed best to come back. I'll take an apartment, find a job —"

"If I can help, let me know."

"Thank you, Cleve. I will."

Cleve hoped that Helen hadn't come back only to find more heartache. Sondra had shut out all of her past.

But still . . . he smiled to himself, remembering the dinner at Antonio's. For a few minutes, she had been like her old self. He remembered her in his arms, the touch of her hair against his face. She had been on the brink that night. One step and she would have been over the edge.

After Helen finished breakfast and said good-bye, Cleve lingered over a last cup of coffee. He was surprised to hear his name being paged. He went to the nearest phone and in a moment was connected with the caller.

"Hello, darling."

"Valerie," he said. "I should have known it was you."

"I want you to come out before you go to the college."

"I'm snowed under with work, Val. I don't want to be late."

"Please. It's important."

"If you want me to speak with Lon Greene again, no thanks."

"No, darling, not that. Remember we were talking once about having a big party, a kind of reunion of all the old crowd? I'd like to talk about that. I've heard rumors that Sondra will be leaving soon. We ought to do it before she goes."

He frowned. It wasn't like Valerie to concern herself with Sondra. What little game was Valerie playing now?

"Can't it wait until tonight?"

"No. Please, come this morning."

He took a deep breath. "All right. I'll be there shortly."

He left the hotel and drove to the DeReuss house, which he always found too fancy and ornate. Ed gloried in it and it was obvious that it suited Valerie.

Valerie was wearing a flimsy negligee, and in anyone's book she was a knockout. Sometimes he forgot just how lovely she was. She came to him and kissed him for a long moment.

"Oh, it's good to see you, darling."

"I can't stay long."

She made a face. "I'm going to keep you forever."

"What's this you're hatching about the reunion?"

"I've got some fabulous ideas. We'll have it at the Wedgewood Inn. We'll plan a gala evening. I'll be in charge."

Cleve smiled. "I see. Then it will be gala."

She laughed, pleased. "Will you dance every dance with me?"

"Why don't you wait and see?"

She led him out to the patio where her breakfast waited. He was surprised to find her father there. Ed DeReuss was a large man with a barrel-sized chest, balding head and horn-rimmed glasses. Cleve began to sense he had walked into a trap.

"Sit down, darling," Valerie said. "Have some coffee."

"I've had my breakfast," Cleve said, setting his jaw.

But he sat down at the table. Ed tossed aside the morning paper, took off his glasses and began to polish

them carefully with a white handkerchief. Beside him, Valerie was patting her foot on the patio floor.

Ed cleared his voice.

"Cleve, I want to talk seriously to you," he said.

Cleve braced himself. "What about?"

"First, I want to make another small donation to the college."

"Thank you. Any donation will be appreciated."

But he knew that Ed was simply paving the way for something else. He was setting him up for the kill, hitting his most vulnerable spot first, the college.

"Have you seen the work at the new clubhouse lately?" Ed asked.

"Yes. It's very impressive."

"Valerie seems to think so," Ed said with a tolerant grin. "I think she's having her problems but she doesn't want me to know about them."

He laughed in an indulgent way.

"It's Valerie's baby but, of course, I'm footing the bills. I aim to get something back from my investment. I think within a year's time the club will have more business than we can handle. It can mean money in the pocket for me, and enjoyment for the people of Lewiston."

Cleve leaned back in his chair. It was plain to see who came first in Ed's eyes.

"The point is this, Cleve. I need a crackerjack of a man to keep an eye on things out there once we get into operation. A general manager who can meet the people, watch the financial end of things, and make it a success."

"That's a big bill to fill," Cleve said carefully.

"But *you* can fill it, Cleve. You handled that matter with Tom Vogel very competently."

Ed paused and looked at him for a long moment for effect. Beside him, Valerie was giving him a smug smile.

"I have my work at the college, Ed. I appreciate the offer but —"

Ed overrode him in his customary manner. "I'll pay you twice what you're getting out there. You'll be in charge and I'll give you a free hand. It's an opportunity of a lifetime."

Cleve's collar began to feel too tight. He resisted the urge to unbutton it and loosen his tie. He began to feel hemmed in, that a gate was closing behind him, that a key was turning in a lock. Something squeezed iron bands around his chest.

"Thank you, no."

Ed reached into his pocket for a cigar, bit off the end and eyed him. "Don't give me an answer now. Think about it. From what I hear, you're going to be my son-in-law one of these days — might as well keep it in the family, hadn't we?"

Like watching a movie in slow motion, Cleve saw himself turning to stare at Valerie. She leaned over and kissed him.

"Don't say no, darling. Please."

"Think it over," Ed said. He got to his feet and towered over them. "I'll be in touch in a few days."

Then Ed was gone. Cleve turned angrily to Valerie.

"You know, I don't like it when you play your little games, Valerie. If you wanted your father to speak with me, why didn't you just say so on the phone?"

"Because you wouldn't have come. Because you're the most stubborn man I ever knew!"

Cleve got to his feet. He was shaking with cold rage. "I

told you once, Valerie, I'm not your little errand boy, nor will I ever be —"

He strode away from the patio and Valerie came running after him. She coaxed and pleaded until finally he stopped and faced her. She buried herself against him and after a moment, he put his arms around her.

"I'm sorry, really, darling, I'm sorry," she said.

"I've got to go."

He pulled open the door, but she stopped him again.

"I *do* mean it about the reunion. I'll work on it right away. Today. I'll invite all the old crowd. We'll have fun. We'll forget all about nasty old business and clubhouses and Daddy —"

He gave her a wry smile. He had heard this song before. For a little while, it would go that way, but sooner or later — it would get back to what Ed DeReuss wanted.

"When are you going to hold this gem of a party?" he asked.

"Why not a week from Saturday night?"

On the way to the college, Cleve took a route that came near Wyler Street. Impulsively, he turned down it toward Carrie's house. He walked up to the wide, front door and rang the bell.

"May I come in?" he asked.

Hesitantly, Sondra opened the door a little wider. He looked around. "Are you alone?"

"Yes. Maxine Davis's granddaughter is very ill. I may have to finish here alone. I was hoping to clear up all the details by the end of the week. Now —"

"Why the hurry?"

She lifted her chin. She gave him a smoky look from her blue eyes. The sunlight came through one of the tall, slender windows and caught the fine gloss of her hair. She

was as lovely as her mother, only in a different way. There was more strength in Sondra's face, more fire in her eyes. He found a sudden and terrible urge to reach out and put his fingers in her hair, to draw her to him, to know her lips once again.

"The hurry is because I want to leave," she said. "The sooner the better."

"You can't go before the reunion," he said. "Valerie wants to have it while you're here."

"What reunion?"

He moved about Carrie's house, touching this and that, and explained. She stood very quietly, watching him, listening.

"You will stay for that, won't you?" he asked. "I'm sure Valerie will be in touch with you."

He spied the hurricane lamp on the spinet. He picked it up and looked at it for a moment.

"It's a lovely thing. Does your offer still hold?"

"Of course," she said stiffly.

But he put it back in place on the piano. She was nervously moving about the room and he knew she wanted him to leave. Beyond the window, he saw leaves stirring in the wind.

"Have you seen DeReuss Park? The color is just starting in the trees."

"No," she said quickly. "I've not been there this trip."

"Stop lying to me, Sondra. Better yet, stop lying to yourself!"

She stared at him, cheeks flushed, eyes wary.

"I want you to go, Cleve. I don't want you to come to this house again!"

He laughed and took a step toward her. She froze, like a frightened deer, and the gesture somehow gave him a

sense of power and strength. The house was so quiet he could hear his heart thudding, the crash of an insect against the window screen.

Three more steps and he was directly in front of her. He reached out to grip her by the shoulders. She was too stunned to react. He bent his head and his lips came down on hers. She did not pull away. For one wild, crazy moment, it seemed she clung to him. Her lips were as he remembered, warm and sweet, fire and ice, thunder and joy.

Then she broke away from him.

"Please go!" she said, tears in her eyes.

"You haven't forgotten me, Sondra. Why do you pretend that you have?"

Then he turned on his heel and walked out of the house, a strange singing in his ears and his heart.

19

SONDRA STOOD very still, not certain that it had happened, that it was real. But she knew that it was, even though it seemed hazy, like something lost in a mist. She did not dare to bring it out into the full light where she would have to look at it and acknowledge it. Nor would she remember what he had said. She forced herself to work.

It was about two o'clock when Maxine Davis stopped by. The poor woman had been crying.

"What is it?" Sondra asked.

"It's little Debbie. There has to be surgery. Serious surgery. It's her heart. We knew she was not as well as she could be, but we didn't realize — oh, I don't know if I can bear it!"

"I'm truly sorry to hear that, Maxine."

"It's going to mean long days in the hospital and still longer days of convalescence at home. It will be more than my son and daughter-in-law can handle alone. I intend to help all I can. It means quitting my job, Sondra. I hate to leave you in a mess like this, but I have to. Please, say you understand."

Sondra nodded. "Yes. Of course. I know how you must feel."

Maxine rushed away. When the door closed behind her, Sondra collapsed into the nearest chair. How could she finish this alone? She knew that Harry was getting more impatient with every passing day.

Oh, there was too much to think about, to do! Her thoughts were pulled in a dozen directions at once. Her emotions had been rubbed raw. Now, each little delay, each question that evaded her, was like salt rubbed into the wound. But somehow Sondra pulled herself together and she went each day to Carrie's house alone, plodding her way through the listing.

It was early Friday morning when Diane Edgar came to Wild Willow, briefcase in her hand.

"Please, tell me!" Sondra said anxiously. "Did you find anything?"

"It's all in the report," Diane said. "I checked every available record I could in Philadelphia. The dates you gave me of Phillip Winterhall's marriage to Tonya Barrett checked out. I was able to locate the apartment house where they lived for a short time. Then the trail grew cold. But I picked it up again and learned they lived abroad."

"Abroad! I didn't know that."

"As a matter of fact, Phillip and Tonya were abroad for about two months."

"And the child?"

Diane accepted the cup of coffee from Sondra and shook her head. "I hesitated to put anything at all in the report. As you know, I work entirely on facts. But I know you were anxious for any information I could get —"

"Yes! Please, tell me!"

"There were rumors that Tonya had a child called Terry. But I don't know if it was a boy or a girl. With that name, it could be either. And my source of information was not clear either."

Sondra sat down with a sigh. "Terry . . ."

"The child was born abroad. Probably in London near the end of World War II. I've sent cables of inquiry. But this is apt to take some time, perhaps a few weeks."

"But you will be able to confirm —"

"I think so."

Sondra felt a letdown sweep over her. Until this moment, she hadn't realized how keyed up she was over all of this. Now the facts were near at hand. It wouldn't be long until Diane gathered the rest of her information.

"I knew it had to be this way!" Sondra said. "I just knew it!"

"But it's not a fact yet," Diane cautioned.

"In your own mind you're practically sure, aren't you?"

Diane took a moment to answer. "I won't say until I'm positive."

"The minute you hear from London —"

"I'll be in touch," she said.

Diane lingered long enough for politeness. Then taking her briefcase, she said good-bye and left. Sondra read the written report several times. Then she phoned Quentin Hancock's office and made an appointment to see him. She knew she would meet opposition from Quentin, but it didn't matter. There was a moral issue here and she couldn't close her eyes to it, no matter what anyone said.

When she went into Quentin's office, she put Diane's report on his desk.

"Please, read this carefully before you say anything," she said.

Quentin frowned as he picked it up and realized what it was. He read it quickly and tossed it aside.

"Miss Edgar has no legal proof of such a birth, Miss Tracy."

"But she'll get it!"

"My answer to that is the same answer it has always been. Carrie Winterhall's will is legal and binding. There is no mention of a grandson. The property and her estate are yours."

Sondra nodded. "I realize that. But don't you understand? I don't want to take something that isn't rightfully mine!"

"I'm not going to argue with you. If Miss Edgar finds solid proof of a grandson, I'll do what I can to contact him. I'll see if we can make some kind of a settlement. Would that satisfy you?"

"Yes."

"All right, then," Quentin said, looking puzzled and a bit angry. "We'll see what develops."

That evening when Sondra went home, she found an invitation to the reunion in her mailbox, written in Valerie's slanting hand. She wasn't sure she would go. Cleve would be there with Valerie hanging possessively to his arm. She didn't want to see him again or remember anything that had happened between them.

Sunday, Gretta invited Sondra to lunch.

"You're fixing enough for an army!" Sondra protested.

"I lose all sense of reason in the kitchen," Gretta laughed.

"What about the hospital. Do you have to make rounds?"

"Not until later."

"Is that all you want out of life, Gretta? To be a good doctor? Don't you want marriage, a home —"

"I'm not sure I'm cut out for that, Sondra. Besides, who would have me?"

"Russ Wagner?"

Gretta flushed. "I think he has eyes for you. You're the romantic, homebody type."

"You don't picture me as a career girl?" Sondra asked.

"I see two pictures. In fact, I've been seeing a new one lately. Have you ever considered staying in Lewiston — now wait, hear me out. You help run an import shop in L.A. I have a hunch you're very good at it. Do you realize we could use such a shop in Lewiston? You'd be perfect for it, Sondra."

"Do you have any other bright ideas?"

Gretta laughed as the doorbell rang. "Yes, I do. Now go and answer that for me, will you?"

Dave Manning stood at the door and beside him, watching her quietly, was Mrs. Tracy.

"Hello, both of you," Gretta said, coming to greet them. She embraced Helen with a quick hug and stretched out a hand to Dave Manning. "It seems like old times, seeing the two of you."

"Ah, we used to have good times, didn't we?" Dave asked.

"The best of times," Gretta said warmly. "Make yourselves at home. I'll be with you in a few minutes. Things are nearly ready."

Sondra followed Gretta to the kitchen.

"Angry?" Gretta asked.

"I wish you had told me you'd invited them."

"I'm sorry if you're so displeased."

"Well, it's your house and your party."

"I know I've poked my nose into your business," Gretta said. "But I *am* fond of your mother, Sondra. Please, can't you try and at least be friends with her?"

"I'll make no promises."

Sondra had simply tried to block her mother out of her thoughts. It was simpler that way. But she would make the best of this encounter for Gretta's sake. She owed her old friend that much.

The lunch was not a huge success. Conversation was stilted at times, despite Dave's efforts to keep it rolling along. But Gretta's manner was quiet and unruffled. Sondra had to admire her poise.

"You'll make some man a great wife, Gretta. First you could feed him like a king and then if he eats too much and gets indigestion, you could take care of that too!" Dave teased. Then he leaned toward Sondra. "Listen, kitten, I've got a good idea. I know Maxine Davis had to quit working. Your mother's at loose ends right now. Why not let her help you at Carrie's house?"

"I do know a little about antiques," Helen said quietly. "And if there's a list to type, I'm not bad."

Sondra mulled it over for a moment. Every instinct said no. But her good sense said yes. It happened to be a very good idea.

"Well," she said slowly. "We might make a trial run, Mother. If you really mean it."

"Oh, I mean it! I'd love to help, Sondra. Thank you. I'll be there Monday morning."

Across the table, Gretta was beaming. Dave was just as pleased. Sondra sighed. At last she had the feeling she'd

done something right, but she wasn't sure, deep down, how it would work out.

Driving back to the lake, Sondra thought about the reunion and decided to drop by the Grandview Hotel to see Lon.

When she reached the hotel, she phoned Lon's room and he said he'd be right down. When he stepped off the elevator a few minutes later, Sondra saw a woman getting off with him. She looked familiar. It took a moment or two to remember where she had seen her before. The Chalet! Yes, that was it. She was the waitress her mother thought looked familiar.

"Hi. This is the nicest thing that has happened all day," Lon said.

"Lon, did you happen to know the woman who came down in the elevator with you?"

"No. But I've seen her around a few times. She visits someone here, I think. Why?"

"No reason."

Lon took her arm and walked with her outside.

"How are things going at the clubhouse?"

"Slow, but sure."

"Valerie DeReuss has good taste. No one can dispute that."

"She can also be a headache," Lon replied.

Sondra laughed. "Then perhaps you wouldn't care to go to a reunion party with me. Valerie has set herself up as hostess."

"Reunion?"

She explained as Lon listened. "You bet I'll go! As long as I don't have to share you too much. Listen, let's take a drive. It's too nice a day to waste."

"The afternoon's nearly gone."

"But there's twilight and evening," Lon said, his blue eyes studying her. "There's dinner —"

They drove away in his station wagon. He skirted the lake, and even for a lovely Sunday, it was not very busy. The season was nearly over. Only a few boats drifted on the blue water.

Lon pulled off to a beach that was more secluded than some. They walked, hand in hand, down to the sand.

"Let's sit here and let the rest of the world go by," Lon said.

The sand was still warm from the sun. The sky was taking on a golden hue, typical of autumn sunsets ' t the lake. Lon picked up a handful of sand and let it sift through his fingers.

"One of these days, the clubhouse will be completed. All of the outside work will be done before we have a hard freeze. Then there will be a few months' work inside — Have you ever been to Dayton, Ohio?"

"No."

"Would you like to go sometime? My family lives there. I'd like them to meet you."

"That would be nice. But more than likely, I'll be returning to Los Angeles before too long."

"You won't stay here?"

"No."

"But you told me once that this is home."

"It *used* to be home," she corrected him quickly. "Home is gone. Cut down by Russ Wagner's bulldozer!"

"You can't blame Russ for that."

"No. But Lewiston's not the same anymore."

"I don't think I ever knew anyone who felt so deeply

for home," Lon said. He leaned toward her. "You're quite a girl, Sondra Tracy."

She got to her feet and walked out to the edge of the water. An egret was startled away and flapped his awkward wings and soared into the sky.

"Such an ugly bird and yet, so graceful —"

Lon came up behind her and put his arms around her. "Don't go back to L.A. I'll have another six months here at least. A lot could happen in six months."

"You're sweet, Lon."

"I want you to think more of me than that," he said.

His blue eyes watched her. His face had tanned and his hair was yellow and curly. There was a vitality about him that was very attractive.

"Let's walk down that way," she said.

He kept her hand and they walked away, kicking sand ahead of them. Beside her, Lon hummed happily and paused now and then to pick up a stone and toss it into the water. The day lengthened. The sun edged down to the treetops and gave the deepening autumn color a tinge of red and gold.

Someone had built a bonfire. The breeze brought back the smoke and Sondra sniffed with a laugh.

"Oh, that makes me think of weiner roasts, DeReuss Park, and raking leaves. A dozen different things. There's no smell on earth quite like it."

"You're a sentimentalist."

"I'm also a fool in many ways," Sondra sighed. "Sometimes, my right hand doesn't know what my left is doing."

"You're talking in riddles."

"Because everything is a riddle for me right now," she said. "Oh, Lon, when do we know when we come full circle? How do we know when things are right for us?"

They stopped walking.

"You're a deep one. I think a man could know you for twenty years and stil learn something new about you every day."

Lon kissed her and she tried to respond. She wanted to float away in ecstasy. She wanted to know that this was where she belonged. She wanted to love Lon Greene. She wanted simply to be whole again.

But as she moved out of his arms with a churning heart, she knew that the answer to her restlessness was not here. It was not with Lon. But if not here, where?

20

Monday morning, Sondra found her mother waiting for her at Carrie's house. Helen was dressed for the work, wearing slacks and a sleeveless blouse, her hair tied in a scarf. She looked surprisingly youthful. Sondra unlocked the door.

"It seems a long time since I've been here." Helen stepped into the large living room and paused, slowly scanning the room with her blue eyes.

"You never came here very often," Sondra pointed out.

"No. Not often. But it's not a place you forget. Besides, you came often enough for both of us."

"I was never allowed to run all over the neighborhood like some children," Sondra said. "But you always let me come here."

"Because I knew Carrie liked to have you. If I had thought for one minute that you were being a bother or a nuisance, I would have put a stop to it. Now, what do you want me to do?"

Sondra showed her the list that had been started, and Helen nodded her head. She picked up a pencil, eager to begin.

They worked silently for a few minutes, then Sondra paused.

"It never occurred to me until this minute that you might have known Carrie's son, Phillip."

Helen brushed back a lock of brown hair. "Yes. I knew Phillip."

"What was he like?"

"Why are you so interested?"

"I'm curious for many reasons. Please, Mother, what was he like?"

"Well, I liked him," Helen said at last. "Some didn't. Some thought he was a show-off. Arrogant. He was that too, but I used to think he acted that way to hide the fact that he was a little unsure of himself."

"And Tonya?"

"Tonya was a wild thing. She came from a family that left a considerable amount to be desired."

"How did Phillip become interested in a girl like that?"

Her mother smiled wryly. "I'm sure it wasn't hard. Tonya was beautiful as well as wild. When Carrie heard Phillip had married her, everyone said she was very upset."

"Mother — did Phillip and Tonya have a child?"

Helen gave her a compassionate look. "Dear, Dave told me about this obsession you have to find Carrie's grandchild."

"This is something I have to do! I've hired a detective. She's found traces of a grandson."

Her mother looked startled. "I don't believe it!"

"No one does, but me. Diane Edgar will soon have positive proof!"

"And if it's true, you intend to do something grand and noble. Oh, Sondra, Sondra —"

Helen shook her head and Sondra decided not to discuss it anymore. They would only argue and the situation between them was already bad enough.

At lunch time, Helen left to meet Dave. Sondra ate alone in a place where she and Cleve used to go. But it had changed so drastically that it gave her a hollow, empty feeling.

She spoke with Gretta on the phone and learned that little Debbie Davis had come through the surgery in fine shape.

The rest of the day, Sondra worked side by side with her mother. They spoke very little. It was just as well. Under other circumstances, it might even have been fun. She was glad when it came time to lock the house and return to Wild Willow, even though she had decided to return for an evening of work as well.

She enjoyed the drive to the cottage. The trees were deepening with autumn color and the air had turned cool.

She made her supper and put it on a tray, pulled a sweater around her shoulders and carried it out to the porch. The sinking sun stained the water and gave the lake a deceptive look of warmth. The leaves had already begun to fall, and here and there wisps of smoke rose above chimneys from the lake houses.

She stirred restlessly and finally went back inside. It was a bad time of day for her. She was always so vulnerable and it was an hour for nostalgia.

She went back to Lewiston earlier than she had intended. She thought of DeReuss Park. Why had she found it necessary to lie to Cleve about visiting there? What could it matter to him now?

She found herself driving there almost against her will. People were having their last flings before cold

weather. Fires blazed in outdoor fireplaces, weiners were roasting, coffee bubbling. She could smell the leaves, see their russets, browns and golds like captured sunlit summer days hanging on for dear life.

Bittersweet Garden was heady with fragrance. Branches were going bare. The stones under her feet felt cold. At the statue, she stared out to the river and saw the twilight turning its waters purple, the first stars shining coldly there in reflection.

"I love you," Cleve had said that time so long ago. "I love you and you're mine and it will never be any different."

"And I love you, Cleve!"

"We're going to be just like the storybooks. We'll be married and live happily ever after."

She had laughed at that. "But first, there's college, and jobs to get and careers to think about — we have to be practical."

"You be practical," he had said. "I'll dream for both of us."

She remembered his kiss, his arms tight around her.

"Oh, stop it!" she told herself fiercely. "Stop it!"

She hurried back to her car and drove as quickly as she could to Carrie's house. The neighborhood on Wyler Street was a quiet one. She pulled into the drive and shut off the motor. Groping for her key, she went up to the front door. She stepped inside the dark house and flipped on a light in the hall.

As she walked into the living room, she paused. A cold chill went over her. She froze in her steps, her hand at her throat. Instinctively, she knew someone had been here, was perhaps still here.

She remembered the time at Wild Willow when she

had suspected someone had been inside. Now, here! She tried the back door. It was firmly locked, just as she had left it. She opened the door and stepped out to the porch. Was that someone running? She listened, ears straining, but in a moment, the sound had died away. Perhaps there *had* been someone there — then again, she wasn't sure.

She went back inside and as she closed the door, she noticed some strange marks around the lock. A scratch or two. Fresh. Her throat went dry. Then she hadn't imagined any of it! Someone had forced his way inside. Someone expert enough to know how to open the lock without breaking it.

She thought of phoning the police. But what use was it now? The prowler had gone. Quickly, she made herself search the house. If there was anything missing, she couldn't see it. Why would anyone break in and then not take anything? Or was it because she had surprised them here too soon?

She thought about Diane Edgar. She made a quick decision and phoned her. In a tense, frightened voice, she explained what had happened.

"I'll come right over," Diane Edgar said.

Sondra paced the room impatiently. When Diane arrived at last, she inspected things in a professional way.

"Why didn't you phone the police?" Diane asked.

"If it gets in the papers that the house is full of valuable antiques, every petty criminal in the city will be trying to break in!"

"Perhaps you're right. Let me dust the back door and the lock for prints. If I find anything I'll run it through the police computer. We might get lucky."

Diane did that and she was elated to find one very clear thumbprint.

"You must have given him a good scare," Diane said. "Otherwise he would have been more careful."

"You'll let me know if the print means anything?"

"Of course. If the print isn't on file here in Lewiston, I'll check further. If the prowler has a record anywhere, I'll find it."

When Diane had gone, Sondra left too. It seemed she couldn't drive away from the house fast enough. She drove home to Wild Willow as if the very devil were in pursuit.

21

THE WEDGEWOOD INN was one of the more attractive night spots around Lewiston and the parking lot was nearly filled when Sondra arrived with Lon for the reunion.

"Is this place always so busy?" he asked.

"Yes," Sondra nodded. "I understand we're to have the Blue Room for the reunion."

"You're excited about this party," Lon grinned. "I had no idea you were sentimental about such things."

"It's always good to see old friends."

"And new ones?" he asked hopefully, leaning toward her with a warm light in his eyes.

"Yes, and new ones," she said.

Lon's arm was solid under her hand. He looked very handsome in his white coat. The invitation had said the affair would be formal. Because most of her things were still in Los Angeles, Sondra had gone out and bought a new evening gown. She had chosen blue. She kept telling herself it was not because Cleve had always liked her in blue, but because the color particularly suited her. Lon had thought so too when he came by for her.

"You're going to be the prettiest girl there," he said with a smile. "And you're my date. How lucky can I get?"

But no one could have held a candle to Valerie DeReuss. She wore a green satin gown that set off her dark hair to perfection. It showed off her lithe figure; the diamonds she wore were real. Beside her, Cleve was tall, attractive, his dark hair brushed, his gray eyes smoldering. Valerie clung to his arm and was never far from his side, exactly as Sondra had expected.

The party got off to a gala start. Everyone came. Gretta was a tiny woman on Russ Wagner's arm, a glow on her face. Russ seemed ill at ease until he came to join Sondra and Lon.

"Hi," he said. "Some party."

"Valerie believes in doing things up right," Lon said. "Where's your date?"

"She saw someone she wanted to talk to," Russ said. "You look great, Sondra."

Lon put a warning smile on his face. "Just remember that she's my date, Russ."

Russ gave him a grin in return. "Worried?"

"Listen, both of you!" Sondra said, embarrassed. "Would you mind not talking as if I weren't even here?"

"All right, then we'll talk business," Lon said. "I expected two more of your men on the job today, Russ, and they didn't come. Mind telling me why?"

"We couldn't make it. As I remember, I didn't definitely promise they would be there."

"And as I remember, you *did* promise!"

"Look, I do the best I can," Russ said, raising his voice.

"So do I. But I have to answer to the DeReuss family. If not Valerie, then Ed himself!"

"Tough," Russ murmured.

Lon was quickly, hotly angry. With alarm, Sondra edged herself between them.

"I think Valerie is about to make an announcement," she said. "Stop acting like little boys."

Valerie DeReuss made a pretty speech, complete with charming gestures, welcoming them all. A small orchestra had been hired, a nice dinner had been arranged and a photographer would move about the room from time to time recording the event for posterity. There were banners, balloons. Valerie made it seem like New Year's Eve.

Sondra was aware from time to time that Cleve was watching her. Once, their glances met, but she looked away quickly, remembering all too clearly the last time they had spoken with each other. Even now, she remembered his arrogant, burning kiss against her lips.

The dinner was superb. Valerie had planned it carefully. There were a few brief speeches from some of the others and a great deal of laughter. Then there was dancing and Sondra went out to the floor with Lon. In a few moments, someone cut in.

Russ Wagner gave them a smile. "It's my turn for a dance. Lon has had you long enough."

"Why don't you butt out?" Lon asked angrily.

Russ kept a grin on his face. "Why don't you?"

"Please," Sondra said with despair. "Will you two stop acting like this?"

"Dance with your own date," Lon said.

"She's busy talking to everybody. Come on, Sondra."

Russ's grip was hard and firm around her wrist. She gave Lon a perplexed, apologetic look and Lon had the good grace to bow out gracefully. Russ pulled her into his arms. The man was always bigger than she remembered,

towering over her. She saw Lon stride across the room and Valerie stopped him. In a moment, they were dancing. Where was Cleve? She saw him then, on the sidelines, still watching her.

"Well, will you go?" Russ asked.

"I'm sorry. What did you say, Russ?" Sondra asked.

He gave her an unhappy frown. "Sondra, I asked you out to dinner tomorrow night."

"Oh. I'm sorry. I can't."

"You're still angry with me. You have been ever since the first time you saw me!"

She laughed. "No. That's silly."

"You don't like me."

"Look, Russ, must we discuss it here? And I wish you'd dance with Gretta. She seldom has a good time. It's a rarity for her to go anywhere but the hospital."

Russ frowned. "She scares me a little."

"Gretta!" Sondra exclaimed. "Why on earth do you say a thing like that —"

"She's a doctor. Educated. Very smart. She's going to be number one in this town before long. I can feel it in my bones. What am I? Nobody from nowhere with dirt under his fingernails most of the time and clay on my boots —"

Sondra laughed. "Russ, you astound me! Do you really think that things like that matter to a woman like Gretta? If you do, you don't know her very well."

Russ shrugged. "I guess I don't at that."

Russ grew quiet as they circled the floor. From across the room, Sondra heard Valerie laughing shrilly. Lon was paying her very close attention and she saw that she had wrapped both arms around Lon's neck and was pressing her cheek to his. Lon looked flushed, uncertain, but he

liked it. Men! Sondra thought with a touch of annoyance. So fickle, so easily twisted around a pretty woman's finger.

Except for one, she told herself. Except for Cleve.

It was almost as if thinking his name, allowing it to creep into her mind, sent wave signals out to him. She saw him leave the sidelines and start through the crowd toward her, elbowing his way through the dancers.

"Russ, let's leave. I mean — I want to go and powder my nose —" Sondra said.

She left Russ standing in the middle of the dance floor. Quickly, hastily, she hurried away, making for the French doors that led to the patio outside the inn. She needed and wanted a breath of fresh air.

She pushed open the doors and stepped out. The cold autumn air stung her lungs, but it cleared her head and gave her a moment to control herself.

Then she heard the doors opening behind her and she spun around. Cleve stood there, the light from the dance floor picking out the dark bow tie, the white coat, the set of his shoulders and the thrust of his chin.

"You've been avoiding me all evening."

"I have nothing to say to you, Cleve."

He laughed, softly, quietly. Then with an abrupt motion, he reached out and took her hand. He tugged her away from the door and the light and down the steps, out across the brick patio floor and into the night.

"Let me go!" she said.

"I want to talk to you. Now, we can do it here where everyone can hear us, or out there, where no one can hear us."

"Won't Valerie miss you?"

"I don't belong to her. I'm not at her beck and call."

"I don't believe that."

He pulled her along until they had reached a large oak tree and there, under the branches that still clung to their brown leaves and would most of the winter, he stopped. He leaned his shoulder against the huge trunk and she heard the dance music, muted now, off in some unreal place.

"Come here," he said.

"No."

He reached out and touched her face, his fingertips tracing the shape of her mouth and then entwining in her hair. She stood as cold and solid as a statue, but the pulse pounded in her throat, a throbbing, wild thing out of control.

He bent his head and pressed his lips there. She touched his dark hair, feeling the smooth texture of it and in a moment, his mouth was on hers, dearly familiar, unlocking the gate, freeing the pent-up love that she had lived with for these long two years. She clung to him, accepting his kiss and giving it back to him, heartbeat for heartbeat, love for love.

Then he let her go and he took a step away from her. There was a triumph to the way he stood, to the sound of his voice, the ring of his laughter.

"You do love me. You've never stopped. I knew you still loved me!"

She understood in that moment the cruel game he had been playing. He had purposely and ruthlessly brought her to her knees. He had ripped open old scars and exposed the beating heart beneath. He had made her face what she had known in the darkness of midnight, in the depths of her soul, in her most silent moments. She had never stopped caring.

But he was making a mockery of it. It meant nothing

now. She had hurt him and he sought to hurt in return. Blindly, she ran from him.

"Sondra, wait —" he called after her. "You don't understand!"

But she did not stop until she reached the French doors. There, she rubbed hastily at her tear-wet cheeks, drew a long, shaky breath and told herself that she would not let this destroy her. She would not run away like a hurt little child. She would finish the party, gaily, laughing, as bright as any star in the sky. She would *show* him.

The party was going noisily ahead, full steam. Everyone was laughing, perhaps drinking a little too much and she saw that Lon and Valerie were still dancing. Neither of them noticed her. Behind her, she heard Cleve come back into the room. She did not look at him. Boldly, she crossed the dance floor and tapped Valerie on the shoulder. Lon looked surprised.

"My turn, Valerie. You've had my man long enough," she said.

Lon's eyebrows shot up and his blue eyes flashed with surprise. But Valerie relented and Sondra moved deep into Lon's arms.

"Hold me close, Lon," Sondra said.

Lon obliged. She did not really hear the music, or remember anything she said or did after that. Not until the party was over at last and she and Lon were driving back to Wild Willow. Lon reached out and held one of her hands tightly.

"Quite a party," he said.

"Oh, yes. Valerie does things in style," she replied.

"Valerie was like a butterfly, flitting from one person to the next. How does a man know when she's serious?"

"When Valerie wants him to know, he'll know," she replied.

"Does she enjoy playing the field so much? It's a wonder a girl like that isn't married already."

"She was married once. It ended in an annulment. It was one of those whirlwind romances. She chooses not to talk about it or even remember it. When you're Valerie DeReuss, you can do that."

By the time Lon reached Wild Willow and walked her to the door, Sondra's head felt as if it were going to burst. Her face was stiff from so much artificial smiling. She was walking a tightrope. Any moment now, she was going to fall off and plunge into the deepest and blackest of seas.

"I've been waiting for a chance to tell you something all evening, Sondra," Lon said. "I heard from my head office. I've already been assigned my new job when I've finished here. In Las Vegas. A real swinging town. We could have a lot of fun there."

Through the haze of her thoughts and the fog that was enveloping her, she heard the word "we."

"I want you to come with me, Sondra."

"Oh, Lon —"

She knew she had led him to believe that she cared. Foolishly, recklessly, she had thrown herself at him tonight after Cleve had made such a fool out of her.

"It's going to be a big job. I'll be there three years, maybe four. I don't want to go alone this time. I want you with me, Sondra?"

He took her hands in his and leaned toward her. His lips touched hers for a moment and then he straightened.

"We'd make a great team, wouldn't we, Sondra?"

"Lon, you're sweet, but —"

"Don't answer right away. Think about it," Lon said.

"You're everything a girl could want, Lon," she heard herself saying, "except —"

"Except, you don't love me," Lon finished for her.

She leaned back, putting her head against the panels of the front door of the cottage and looked at his face in the starlight.

"I'm sorry."

"Is there someone else?" he asked in a somber voice.

She swallowed hard. It was almost impossible to get the word past her throat, to allow herself to say it. For two years, it had been locked away so deep she had pretended it didn't exist. Now, she knew the truth.

"Yes, someone else," she said.

Lon stood very quietly for a moment, looking at her. "He's a lucky guy," he said. Then he nodded and said good-night.

Sondra was too thoughtful to sleep. She struck a match and touched it to the wood in the fireplace, waiting for it to catch. When the flames were rushing upward, crackling fiercely, she sat down on the sofa to watch them.

"I still love Cleve," she said aloud. "I will always love Cleve. But now — he surely hates me. And I can't blame him."

22

SONDRA DID NOT KNOW how long she sat before the fire. She knew the logs had nearly burned down to ashes when she finally went to bed. Her head had barely touched the pillow when the phone rang. She thought of not answering it. It might be Lon, deciding to be persistent, or crazy, mixed-up Russ Wagner or even — Cleve? No. It wouldn't be Cleve. When the phone kept ringing insistently, she finally got up and went to answer it.

It was long distance, and soon she heard Harry Chapman's voice.

"Hello, Sondra. I've been trying all evening to reach you."

"I was out. Do you know how late it is?"

"Yes. But it's two hours earlier here. Sondra, I've got to ask you to come back. On the next plane. It's an emergency. I must see you."

"But Harry, I've not finished matters here —"

"You don't understand. It's urgent!"

"Harry, what is it? What aren't you telling me?"

"It concerns the shop. I have to talk to you but not over

the phone. Will you come right away? I know it's a bad time for you, but this won't take long."

She knew Harry well enough to know that if he was putting this much stress on it, it had to be important. The least she could do was cooperate. Harry had been patient with her for so long.

"All right, Harry. I'll come tomorrow."

He hung up, leaving a dozen questions in her mind.

The next morning, Sondra arranged to meet her mother for breakfast.

They met in a little coffee shop downtown. Her mother was there and waiting, eyes filled with questions. "Something's happened."

"I didn't realize it showed," Sondra said.   ·

Mother gave her a wistful smile. "I know you better than you think, Sondra."

"Do you?"

"Yes."

"Well, that's neither here nor there right now. I had a phone call from Harry last night. I don't know exactly what's up but he wants me back there right away. I'm going to take the ten o'clock flight. The thing is, I'll need you to continue work at the house. Would you do that for me, Mother?"

Her mother reached out and covered Sondra's hand for a moment. "Don't worry about a thing. I'll handle it. If I run into any problems, I'll consult Quentin Hancock."

The flight was uneventful. Sondra sat beside the window and watched the earth slipping away beneath her, stared at the fleecy clouds and wondered at the beauty of the Grand Canyon when they passed over it. Then Los

Angeles came into view and she braced herself for whatever calamity awaited her.

A cab took her to Imports, Inc. She opened the door and paused for a moment. Oh, it was nice to be back. She loved this shop!

Harry heard her and came out from the back room. He gave her a welcoming grin.

"Glad you got here so fast."

"But what is it? You scared the wits out of me. I imagined all sorts of things. I thought you were sick or the shop had been burned down or —"

Harry grinned. "Nothing like that. But we've got to talk. Come on back to the office."

The office had grown cluttered in her absence. She frowned at the desk, littered with paper and knew that Harry had dropped back into his old, bad habits.

"I'll put it right on the line, Sondra," Harry said. "I've had an offer for this shop. A very good offer."

Sondra straightened with surprise. "An offer! You mean you're going to sell out?"

"I mean I'm getting out of the business. I'm sixty-five. I want to quit. It's time I quit. Now, here's the situation. I can sell to an interested party, take my money and go. Or, I can sell half interest to you, keep the other half as an investment. I've been thinking of making you a partner for a long time anyway. You've got the stuff, Sondra, and it's a real opportunity for you."

"You're really making it hard, Harry."

Harry nodded. "I know it's putting the squeeze on you at a bad time. But think about it. The thing is, I've got to have my answer by tomorrow morning. Ten o'clock. I have to let the other people know by then."

"But, Harry, how can I decide that fast?"

Harry leaned toward her, talking rapidly, giving her a fast sales pitch. He named figures, inventory valuation, possible changes she might want to make, and before she knew it he had her head spinning.

"Wait a minute," she said, holding up her hand. "You're going too fast for me, Harry. You've got to give me some time to think —"

"You got all the time in the world — up until ten o'clock tomorrow morning."

She picked up her purse and moved to the door. "I just don't know —"

She left the shop, hailed a cab, went to her apartment and let herself in.

The apartment was comfortable, even a little stylish, with modern furniture and a view of the city. After rustic, cozy Wild Willow, it was almost a different world. She had not been ecstatically happy here, coming as she had from Lewiston with clouds hanging over her head, but it had served her well enough. But what should she do now?

It would be so simple to stay here and take over the shop. She could forget Lewiston and everyone there. Still, there was the problem of Carrie's grandson. But if Diane Edgar succeeded in finding him, she could always fly back for a day or two and take care of things.

But what about Wild Willow, the town of Lewiston itself? What about Carrie's house? What about home — oh, but home was gone! She must remember that.

She had made her break. Why go back now? If she stayed, wouldn't it be an easy way out of everything? She would never have to see the mockery on Cleve's face again.

She thought of phoning some of her friends in Los

Angeles. Perhaps a night out would help her decide. But she didn't touch the phone. She paced the apartment, then spent a frantic hour or two with paper and pencil. It was a good investment. She knew she could be successful running the shop alone.

But did she want to stay in Los Angeles or go back to Lewiston? That was what she had to decide and soon.

When the phone rang about eight o'clock that evening, she fully expected it to be Harry. She was surprised instead to hear Gretta's voice.

"What's wrong?" Sondra asked. "I know you're not calling just to be sociable."

"How are things out there?"

"In a quandary."

"When will you come home?"

"I'm not sure I am coming home, Gretta."

"I wish you would. It's Nona Campbell. I had to hospitalize her this afternoon. She's had a coronary. Her condition is grave. She keeps asking for you."

"Me! But why?"

"There seems to be something she wants to tell you. She gets almost hysterical about it. Could you come back? On the very first flight? There isn't much time."

Sondra clenched the phone tightly. She knew perfectly well what Nona wanted to tell her. It was something about Carrie's grandson. But what about Harry and the shop? What was she going to do about that?

"I'll see what I can do, Gretta."

It took only a moment or two for Sondra to decide. She reached for the phone again and dialed Harry's number.

"Sondra! You've decided," he said.

"There's no way you could delay my decision?"

"Not a chance," he said. "Why?"

"Then it will have to be no. I must go back to Lewiston. It's an emergency."

"But, Sondra, do you know what you're doing?"

"Yes. It was a choice between two important things · and Lewiston won out."

Harry was a long time in replying. "I'm sorry to hear that. I was hoping — but, well, you know what you want to do."

"Harry, I appreciate the offer more than you can know. It was great working for you. I loved the shop —"

"Sure," Harry said. "I understand."

Sondra caught the first flight available and had breakfast on the plane somewhere over Denver. By the time she reached Lewiston, her nerves were in a fine nettle.

Gretta was there to meet her.

"How is Nona, Gretta?"

Gretta shook her head slowly. "I'm not sure she'll last the day. But she's still conscious. She still asks for you."

"Let's go. Quickly," Sondra said. "I won't wait for my luggage now. I'll pick it up later."

A NO VISITOR sign was on the hospital door, but Gretta took her in. Nona's eyes were closed but Gretta awakened her gently.

"Nona, can you hear me?"

"What?" she asked weakly. "What?"

"Nona, Sondra Tracy is here. You wanted to see her, remember?"

The old woman seemed to brighten. Her eyes opened. Sondra bent over her with a smile.

"Hello, Nona."

"Glad you could come," she said. "I want to talk to you — alone . . ."

Gretta nodded and stepped out into the hall. Sondra took Nona's hand in hers.

"Now, what did you want to tell me?"

"You asked me, about Carrie's grandchild."

Her voice was very low, barely audible. Sondra leaned closer to hear her.

"Yes. Tell me about it, please."

"I lied to you. Had to keep my promise . . ."

"I understand, Nona."

"There *was* a grandchild. A grandchild that Carrie loved . . ."

Nona's voice faded away. Sondra leaned closer. "Nona — Nona — keep talking. Tell me about the grandchild. Where is he?"

But Nona had closed her eyes. She didn't seem to hear her. Sondra rushed out to the hall.

"Gretta! Please — come —"

Gretta took one look. "Nona can't talk anymore, Sondra."

"Is she —"

"Unconscious," Gretta said sadly. "It won't be long now . . ."

23

Helen tracy was surprised to receive a phone call from Sondra about five o'clock that afternoon. She was at the hospital, hoping Nona Campbell would rally. But there seemed to be little hope. Gretta had finally told her to go home.

"Would you mind driving me out to Wild Willow, Mother?" Sondra asked.

"Of course not. I was just about to leave here."

Helen locked Carrie's house carefully and then drove to the hospital. She was shocked to see how tired her daughter looked.

"Nona isn't any better?"

"No."

"But why have you come all the way back to Lewiston for an old woman you hardly know?" she asked.

"Simple. Nona wanted to tell me something about Carrie's grandchild. So you see, he *does* exist, just as Diane Edgar believes, just as I believe!"

Helen gripped the wheel tightly. "And did Nona —"

"She lost consciousness before she could tell me any-

thing except that there is a grandchild. I think she knew much more than that — if only . . ."

"I see," Helen said. "Is there any hope for her?"

"Gretta says not. Oh, what a pity! Why didn't I ask her sooner? Why didn't I persist? If there was more to be learned —"

Helen reached over and clasped her daughter's hand for a moment and found it cold.

"How did you leave things in Los Angeles? What was the emergency?"

"Everything's settled there," Sondra replied.

She didn't seem to want to discuss it further and Helen didn't pry.

Sondra put her head back and closed her eyes. Sometimes her daughter's beauty came as a total surprise to Helen. The girl had turned out so well. She was fiercely proud of her, much more than Sondra knew or she could ever tell her. Perhaps someday they could be close. She longed for that.

They stopped by the airport for Sondra's luggage and then drove straight to Wild Willow. When they reached the cottage on the lake, they found it uncomfortably chilly.

"I see Tom Vogel has the wood box filled," Sondra said. "I think I'll build a fire."

"How about some coffee? I'll make it."

"Yes. I'd like that."

Sondra brought in an armful of firewood, heaped the kindling and struck a match. In a few minutes, the fire was blazing warmly, taking the chill off the room. Sondra gripped the mantle with both hands and stared down into the flames. She was a picture of unhappy loneliness and Helen's heart was touched.

"Dear, I have a snack ready. Why don't you eat here, in front of the fire?"

Sondra nodded. "Fine, Mother. Thank you. Aren't you joining me?"

"No. Dave's taking me out for a late dinner."

The fire snapped and crackled, and outside the window, the blackness of an autumn night wrapped around the cottage.

Sondra drank three cups of the hot coffee but barely tasted the sandwich Helen had made for her. She was troubled. Restless. She jumped up often to poke at the fire and walked around the cottage, touching this or that, talking very little. Helen's heart went out to her. She wanted to stay, but she sensed that Sondra needed to be alone.

"Will you be all right, Sondra?"

Sondra nodded. "Yes. Thank you, Mother. For everything."

"I'll come by in the morning and pick you up."

"All right," Sondra nodded.

Helen wanted in the worst way to draw her daughter to her and kiss her as she used to when she was a small girl, but she knew she couldn't do that now. Sondra would resist and be embarrassed by the gesture. Sondra had never truly forgiven her. Perhaps she never would until she knew the entire story. It was a story Helen didn't want to tell her, but perhaps she would have to.

Helen drove back to the hotel. She had yet to find an apartment. She had been so busy working at Carrie's house there had been little spare time for apartment hunting.

When Dave Manning came by at eight, she hurried to let him in.

Dave smiled at her and reached out both hands.

"Dave — it's good to see you."

"Sweet music to my ears," he laughed.

He drew her close. His lips were warm and tender. He held her close for a moment.

"I love you, Helen. You must know that. I love you so very much."

"Dave, you're so sweet, so good to me!"

"I cherish you. I've always cherished you. Even when you were Arnold's wife, I loved you. I thought you knew, that you sensed it."

"Yes, I think I did."

"Have you told Sondra about us?" he asked.

"No. I thought I would when I drove her to Wild Willow this afternoon, but I couldn't. She seemed so tired and upset. I hadn't the heart."

"Do you think she'll mind? She's very fond of me and you know how I feel about her."

Helen shook her head. "I can't predict how she'll take anything these days, Dave. She's so confused, so unhappy, so wrought up —"

Dave touched her cheek with a gentle hand. "I think she should be told. Right away. Before she hears it from someone else."

Helen shook her head. "Please, Dave, let me handle it in my own good time."

"Anything you want," Dave said. "Now, let's have dinner. We've a great deal to talk about."

Dave treated her so well that it was a joy to be with him. He made her feel important, wanted. It had been a long time since she'd felt like this. Arnold Tracy had been in love with her. They'd had good times as well as bad.

But there had always been a shadow between them that Arnold had never been quite able to erase, a shadow that had finally come between them.

"Only the best will do for my girl," David said, as they sat in the Wedgewood Inn. "Helen, I know you want to wait, but I've already waited so long. Let's set a date to be married."

Helen hesitated. She wanted to marry Dave. She loved him. To find that she could care so deeply for him so quickly surprised her. But she trusted her feelings. Dave had been a part of her life for years. She had always been fond of him. She had always known in the back of her mind that he cared more than a little for her, but he had been gentleman enough to keep it to himself. She respected and honored him for that.

"My secret love," he said, teasingly. "Now I can tell everyone. I *want* to tell everyone, very soon, Helen."

"Dave, my life has not been perfect. I've made some bitter mistakes. I've done some things I'm not proud of —"

"Haven't we all?"

"But you don't understand, Dave. There are things I should tell you —"

"No explanations are needed for anything. It's as simple as this. I love you, Helen. Nothing else matters. Imagine, me marrying you. When we were young, you were one of the most popular girls in the crowd. Every boy was crazy about you."

She smiled. "That's going back a few years, Dave."

"Arnold was always wild about you. But you were a long time in making up your mind. As I remember, you dated a lot of different fellows. Johnny Saffron. Remem-

ber him? And Duke Edwards. I think you even went around with Phillip Winterhall a few times. Then there was Frank Frazer. My trouble was, I didn't know at the time I was going to fall in love with you or I'd have been in there pitching for your attention too."

"You make me sound like the belle of the ball and I wasn't."

"Yes, you were. I remember when you left town for a while. Went East or someplace. Before I knew it, Arnold went chasing after you. Brought you back. Married you. Then there was little Sondra — the light of my eyes!"

She shook her head. "Oh, Dave, let's not go back. Let's think ahead. I'd like to forget everything in the past and simply start new."

Dave reached out and took her hand in his. "I'm all for that, darling. As long as I can face tomorrow with you."

"I don't deserve you, Dave. But I want a new life. A chance to be worthy of you, a chance to erase and forget old mistakes —"

"All you have to do is name the day," Dave said with a smile. "The sooner the better."

He made it sound so easy. She wanted to do just that. Name the day! Forget everything else. But she knew she couldn't start a new life so simply, so easily. Sometime, she would have to tell him the things about her that he didn't know. Things that might matter. But she prayed they wouldn't. For she loved Dave. She needed him. He was the open door she had been looking for. Beyond was the rainbow, waiting.

After they'd eaten, Dave suggested a drive.

"Around the lake, or wherever you want to go."

"Not the lake," she said.

Seeing the lake would remind her of Sondra. She wondered anxiously about Nona Campbell. Would the old woman rally and tell Sondra still more?

They drove for a long stretch out into the country, past fields rich with harvest, then down a winding lane and finally back toward the city.

"We could run away," Dave said. "Like two kids. Just go and very simply tie the knot."

Helen laughed. "Don't tempt me."

"I'll tempt you every time I see you," Dave promised. "You can bet on it."

Dave saw her to her room. He kissed her tenderly.

"No fools like old fools?" she asked lightly.

"We're not that old. And we're not fools. I'm a man and you're a woman and we belong together. It's as simple as that. Promise me you'll talk to Sondra soon."

"Soon," she nodded.

Then Dave was gone.

She leaned against the window and watched the city below. Lewiston! Home. Dave was a good man. He would make her happy. Still . . .

She turned away from the window. She couldn't think about it now, although she knew that she would have to think about it soon.

She went to bed late and had just dropped off to sleep when the phone awakened her.

"Sondra? What's wrong?"

"I just had word from the hospital. Gretta phoned. Nona's gone. A few minutes ago."

Helen was fully awake now. "I see. I'm so sorry."

"Yes. So am I."

"Did she — I mean —"

"She didn't talk anymore. I'll never know what else she meant to say."

"Best to forget it, dear."

"I *can't* forget it!" Sondra said with anger. "Don't you understand that? There *is* a grandson and I've got to find him!"

24

THE NEXT MORNING, Sondra made her breakfast and lingered by the window overlooking the lake. Gretta's phone call last night from the hospital was still very fresh in her mind. Poor Nona! What secret had she taken with her? All Sondra could do now was wait for Diane Edgar's final report.

Sondra heard a car pull into the drive. It was Lon Greene.

"Good morning! I noticed your light last night and knew you were back," Lon said.

"Why aren't you on the job?" Sondra smiled.

"Things are going more smoothly now. They can spare me for half an hour or so. How are you, Sondra?"

"A little tired. Perhaps this jet travel doesn't agree with me. What's been happening while I was away?"

"Well, for one, Valerie has really been setting the fire under me. Trying to hurry along the construction. She can be quite effective," Lon said with a frown. "But at least Russ came through. He's down there this morning, personally running one of his machines. I'm glad of it. This weather isn't going to last forever."

"Winter's coming," Sondra said. "Time to get things done. I must speak to Tom Vogel about helping me get the storm windows ready for the cottage."

Lon gave her an inquiring look. "The other night, Sondra, when I told you about Las Vegas, you said no. Any chance you've changed your mind?"

"No. I'm sorry, Lon."

"I suppose it sounded like a half-baked idea at that. Maybe it was. It just sort of popped out."

She was amused. "Are you trying to say you want to take back your proposal?"

Lon lighted a cigarette and shook out the match. "Well, not exactly, but I don't want to rush into anything either. I feel a little foolish saying so now."

"I know how it is," she said with a sigh. "In the summertime things look different than they do in the fall. Summer is a time for fun, for crazy ideas, for reckless thoughts — but somehow when we face them in the cold light of winter . . ."

Lon smoked his cigarette. They talked about the lake and the families who had summer cottages there. Most of them had closed their places and gone. There were only a few that wintered there.

They heard the sound of a car going by and Lon caught a glimpse of it out of the window.

"It's Valerie," he said. "Heading for the clubhouse. Which probably means she wants something else changed."

A little later, Sondra was talking with Tom Vogel.

"If you're looking for more work, I was thinking about the storm windows."

Tom nodded. "The time's right. Where are they stored?"

"In the garage, I think. I'll come out and we'll look."

She unlocked a storage area in the garage and Tom pulled out the windows.

"They're a mess. Take some scrubbing. This one needs some putty too," Tom said.

"Make a list of anything you need, Tom. I'll pick it up in town later. Would you have time to drive me to the car rental agency?"

"Oh, sure thing," Tom nodded. "Anytime you want to go."

"Tom, you're an angel. I don't know what I'd do without you."

Tom frowned and shook his head. "I don't know, Miss Tracy. I keep thinking surely I'll remember something really important."

"Well, perhaps, if nothing comes back to you today — then tomorrow," Sondra said, trying to sound hopeful.

About an hour later, she asked Tom to drive her to Lewiston. He had made a list of things he'd need to put the storm windows in good repair and she gave him enough money to buy them.

It was a clear, bright day but cool. Beside her, Tom was whistling softly.

"You know, Miss Tracy, I noticed that old table stored out in the garage. I bet it's solid walnut. If you wouldn't mind, I'd like to take off the old varnish and refinish it. It would look great in front of your fireplace. We might even fit it with some of those funny feet. You know they look like animal claws and there's a big glass ball underneath."

"Yes, I know what you mean. How do you know about such things, Tom?"

Tom frowned and laughed softly. "Darned if I know, Miss Tracy. But it seems I remember a table with feet like that. It had a little drawer in it and marble on the top. And inside, there was some kind of sachet. Smelled good. The left front leg was loose. Wobbly. Should have been fixed a long time ago — "

Tom broke off. "Listen to me! Now can you beat that? I don't know what I'm talking about — but I do know I remember a table like that. If only I could remember where I'd seen it."

Sondra felt a ripple of nerves run along her arms. The table in Carrie's house. The front left leg was loose on that one too. Inside was an envelope of lavender sachet — Carrie's favorite scent. Tom Vogel had described it perfectly.

"You're sure you don't remember where you saw such a table, Tom?" she asked carefully.

"No. Except that it was a long time ago. When I was a kid. Well, here is the rental agency, Miss Tracy. Is there anything else I can do for you?"

Sondra shook her head. She climbed out of the car.

"No. Thank you, Tom."

Tom gave her a smile. Then, whistling, he drove on.

Lon Greene had caught up with Valerie DeReuss before she reached the building site. Valerie was wearing an orange dress that suited her nearly as well as the green evening gown she wore at the reunion party.

"You're out early," Lon said.

Valerie smiled at him as he held the car door. "How's it coming?"

"Good," he said. "We're back on schedule, in fact a little ahead."

"Would you have time to take me on a tour?"

"Of course."

He always felt some measure of pride in his work. This had not been the easiest job; there had been all sorts of unforeseen problems. But now he felt he could relax a little.

Valerie asked a great many questions. She squinted prettily in the bright sunlight and occasionally he gave her his hand to help her walk among the building materials and over the rough ground which had not yet been smoothed by one of Russ Wagner's machines.

"Oh, I can just see it, Lon," Valerie said with a happy laugh. "It will be the swankiest place in Lewiston."

"It's going to be great," Lon agreed. "I hope I can get back for the grand opening."

Valerie gave him a quick glance. "You won't be here?"

"It's doubtful. Las Vegas is my next stop."

"What a shame! It's been so nice having you around," Valerie said.

Her voice was purring. It was probably an act, one she put on for any man. But he couldn't seem to make himself believe that.

"Let's have some coffee over at the Grandview," Lon said. "I'll tell you about my plans. And I'd like to hear yours. What else besides a clubhouse do you have up your sleeve?"

"You'd never guess."

"That sounds intriguing."

She took his arm as they walked to the hotel and went into the coffee shop. Most of the summer people had gone. Only a few regulars were still at the hotel.

"I didn't realize it was so cold out," Valerie said, holding her coffee cup with both hands.

Lon reached out and took both her hands in his.

"I'll warm them," he said.

"Likely excuse," she laughed. "Why don't you just admit you want to hold my hand?"

He grinned at that. "Okay, so it's a nice idea. Do you object?"

She thought for a moment, a teasing smile on her lips. "No. I don't think so."

"Then let's go one step farther. Let's have dinner tonight."

"I'm not sure I could go tonight."

Lon frowned. "Cleve Ridgeway?"

Valerie's eyes flashed. "Perhaps. I'm never certain any more. Cleve always seems to be busy —"

"Since Sondra Tracy got back to town?" Lon asked.

"You know about them?"

"Yes. I know a great deal about you too, Valerie."

"You don't know anything!" she protested.

"Fact one. You're the richest girl in town. You're probably also the prettiest. You've had several love affairs. None of them seem to work out."

Valerie was watching him warily. "What's all this to you?"

"You're looking for someone, Valerie. The right man. Who knows — maybe that someone is me."

Valerie was amused. But she wasn't laughing. He had struck a chord.

"Talk about male chauvinism . . ."

He smiled and squeezed her hands. "Faint heart never won fair lady. Now, how about it? Dinner tonight?"

"It might be fun," she said. "All right."

"Let's start the evening right now."

He leaned across the table. She met him halfway and their lips met. She smelled of perfume and fresh air and she tasted of ecstasy.

They lingered for a long time over their coffee. It grew cold in their cups. Suddenly, there was so much to say to each other . . .

. . . and almost as suddenly, Lon's foreman came into his hotel. Lon frowned. It probably meant some kind of trouble, but he didn't want to be interrupted now.

"Boss —"

"What is it?" Lon asked impatiently.

"There's been an accident. One of the machines —"

Lon was on his feet, blood draining out of his face.

"What machine? What driver?"

"Russ Wagner. It flipped on him. I'm afraid he may be hurt real bad."

25

GRETTA BERGLUND had already put in a busy morning,
She had made hospital rounds early and was pleased to
find that Maxine Davis's little granddaughter, Debbie,
was doing very well. From all indications the heart surgery
had been successful.

She was midway through her morning office appointments when her nurse called her to the phone.

"Emergency, Dr. Berglund. Lon Greene is on the line."

She picked up the receiver.

"Gretta! There's been another accident! I've phoned an
ambulance. He'll be on his way soon. Could you meet
him at the hospital?"

"Slow down, Lon. Who's been hurt?"

"Russ. Russ Wagner! One of those big machines of his
turned over. He tried to jump clear, I think, but it caught
him and wedged him underneath. We had a hell of a time
getting him free. He's out cold. I'm afraid —"

Gretta was used to emergencies. They happened every
day in her profession. It was always possible that Lon was
overly excited, that he was mistaken as to the seriousness

of the accident. But whenever Gretta remembered those huge machines Russ had . . .

It was a bright, cool day with a breeze blowing. The leaves were nearly all down and earlier, over breakfast, she thought she'd seen a touch of frost on the rooftops. At the Lewiston Hospital, Gretta put her car in the doctors' reserved area and went in through a side door. By the time she reached Emergency, she heard the siren. In a few minutes, the attendants brought Russ in.

"It's a bad one, Dr. Berglund."

She bent over Russ. For a moment she touched his dark curly hair. His breathing was shallow and irregular. His color alarmed her.

"Were you there when they freed him?" she asked.

"Yes. Lucky, when he jumped, he landed in sand. Otherwise, he'd be dead by now. He took a hard blow around the chest area. I think he's got a broken leg, too."

Gretta nodded. She was cutting away Russ's shirt, exposing the bleeding flesh beneath it. She feared a punctured lung and other internal injuries.

It took nearly half an hour for her to make a thorough examination. She ordered Russ taken to X ray. After she'd read the pictures, she would know for certain what must be done.

Lon was pacing up and down the hall, smoking a cigarette. When he saw her, he came rushing over.

"How is he?"

"Still unconscious. There's internal bleeding. Probably several broken ribs, a possible punctured lung and other internal injuries."

Lon shook his head with despair. "What a lousy thing to happen!"

"If you know his family, they should be called."

"No. I don't. But I'll find out from some of his men. I'll take care of it, Gretta."

"Just remember that Russ is a strong man. With luck, he'll come through this easier than we might expect right now."

"Anything he needs, get him, Gretta. Any medication, or special nurses or special doctors — get it for him. Our company's insurance will take care of all of it."

"I'm not a surgeon, Lon. If one is needed —"

"Get the best. Whoever you recommend," Lon said. "And of course — whatever his family says about such things —"

"There's a possibility there won't be time to consult his family unless they are reached soon."

Lon eyed her. He ran a shaky hand over his blond hair and looked pale. "I see."

Gretta tried to give him a reassuring smile. "Give it twenty-four hours. I'm sure things will be much improved by then. Now, if you'll excuse me —"

"Sure. But I'll be back, as soon as I make some phone calls."

Gretta nodded and walked away. She went up to X ray and waited. Russ was rushed through; the moment Gretta had the pictures, she studied them for a long time. What she found gave her a cold, clammy feeling in the pit of her stomach.

Looking at her watch, she knew that Lon had been gone about forty-five minutes. She couldn't wait any longer. She alerted the OR and then put in a call to Dr. Bradford. He was the best surgeon in town for this kind of work. He was slow, but very thorough. He could put Russ back together if anyone could.

Lon reappeared shortly after Gretta had made arrangements.

"No luck. Wouldn't you know it? Russ's mother has gone to California to visit a daughter. I reached a brother and he'll be here as soon as possible, but the word is — do what you think best."

"I've already called in Dr. Bradford and we'll be taking Russ to surgery as soon as we can get him ready."

"I see," Lon said.

"I'll let you know how it goes."

Lon disappeared down the hall and Gretta saw him stop at a phone booth. She had no idea whom he was calling now. It hardly mattered. She would scrub and assist Dr. Bradford. She wanted to see with her own eyes what was found and what was done.

Gretta phoned her office to alert them that she would be tied up for several hours. When she hung up, she saw Sondra coming down the hall, walking swiftly, an anxious look on her face.

"Lon called me," she said. "How bad is it, Gretta?"

Gretta shook her head. "I can't really be sure until Dr. Bradford finishes. But there is internal bleeding and it's not getting any better."

"Gretta, he *is* going to be all right," Sondra said.

Gretta blinked fast. "He *has* to be!" She paused. "Well, I must go. They'll be operating soon."

"Keep the faith, hon."

Gretta nodded and walked away, hands held rigidly in the pockets of her white coat. Keep the faith! How many times had she done that as a doctor, as a person? Now, she must do it again. This time, it was probably more important than it ever had been before.

There had never been anyone in her life that she had

truly been serious about. Perhaps because there had never been time. It had always been work, work, work. By taking extra credits, she had finished high school early. She had never stopped going to school when she was working for her M.D. A summer vacation had been an unheard-of luxury. But the sacrifice had gotten her through quicker, enabled her to set up her office and start practicing a year ago.

To find herself in love with a man like Russ Wagner now came not only as a surprise but as a shock. But she couldn't let herself think of that now.

Dr. Bradford arrived and made straight for the operating room. Gretta briefed him as they scrubbed, giving him all the information she had and together they looked at the X rays. As they prepared to go to surgery, Gretta paused. For a moment, she said a prayer. Then she made herself become a doctor instead of a woman. She went inside to the greenish glare of the lights of the operating room and took her place beside the surgeon.

The surgery was lengthy. But Russ held up splendidly and they were grateful for his strong heart and hardy constitution. Bradford was neat and thorough, and it was a bone-weary three hours before they were finished. Gretta changed from OR greens to a white coat.

She left the hospital and drove back to her office where afternoon patients were still waiting. She would see as many as she could, but the rest would probably have to come another day. She was glad to be kept busy. Every time the phone rang, she held her breath. But there was no word about Russ and she began to feel easier. About four o'clock, she checked with the nurse on the floor as to his general condition and was satisfied with the information.

By six she had seen her last patient and was free to return to the hospital.

Russ had been settled in his own room. He was still getting blood intravenously and he was conscious. When she bent over him, he opened his eyes.

"Hi," he said.

"I don't want you to talk. Just rest. Okay?"

"Will I be all right?"

"Of course!"

He closed his eyes again and sighed. "Don't lie to me. I know I'm hurt real bad."

"Sleep. Rest. Save your strength," Gretta said. "You'll be all right."

He reached out and clutched her hand. "Will you be here, Gretta?"

"I'll be here," she said.

He tried to smile. Then he dropped off into a deep sleep once again. Gretta pulled a chair close and sat down. She would stay as long as she could.

26

SONDRA WAS AT THE HOUSE on Wyler Street. She had already looked at the small table in the front hallway, the one with the loose leg and the bag of lavender sachet inside the drawer. Tom Vogel had described one like it perfectly!

Could it have been just a coincidence? That question plagued her as she tried to put the last of the list down on paper. It plagued her on the drive back to Wild Willow. It was still on her mind that evening, when Dave and her mother dropped by unexpectedly. For a while the three talked about Russ Wagner. Sondra suggested they stay for dinner.

"No, thanks," Dave said.

Sondra looked from one to the other, sensing that something was in the wind.

"Look, I think I'll take a quick stroll down to the dock," Dave said.

Almost before he had come inside, he had gone again, and Helen Tracy was pacing about restlessly.

"You're making me nervous, Mother. Why don't you sit down?"

"I just don't know how to tell you this."

"Tell me what?"

"About Dave. We're going to be married. There, I've said it!"

Sondra stared at her mother, at a loss for words. She had half expected this, but not so soon.

"I know how you felt about your father," her mother said uneasily. "You two were always so close. Dave understands that as well as I do. He doesn't want to take Arnold's place, nor will he try. But he cares for you, Sondra. He always has. We want your blessing."

"My blessing!" Sondra echoed.

"I know this seems sudden. But he has promised to make me happy. I only hope I can do as much for him."

"When you didn't for Dad?" Sondra asked, a trace of the old bitterness in her voice.

Helen blinked fast and looked away. "Dear, I did what I could. There were good times, too, if you'll remember. I'll never forget your father, Sondra, and what he did for me. He came to me at a very difficult time of my life — a time when I needed him, and for that, I'll always be grateful. But I don't want to look back, I want to look ahead."

Sondra sighed tiredly. "Yes. We should all do that, shouldn't we?"

"Then you wish us luck?"

"Yes," Sondra said. "Of course I do."

When Dave came back in, he sensed her mood.

"Remember, when I told you I had a secret love?" He took her hands in his for a moment. "Well, I've loved your mother for many years. Even when she was married to your father. I never told her so, but she knew. She

never once acknowledged it nor did she make me uncomfortable because of it. That takes a special kind of lady, Sondra, and that lady is your mother."

He seemed so anxious for her approval.

"Your father was my best friend, Sondra. You're already the same as a daughter to me. Let us be happy together."

She laughed and reached up to kiss him.

"Let's go to the Chalet. Right now. For a special dinner. My treat. To celebrate."

Dave's eyes were shining with happiness. "That's my girl!"

The supper was a huge success. Sondra even felt warmly toward her mother. As for Dave, she had always loved him anyway. Dave made several toasts and Sondra hoped all the joyful things he proposed would come true.

They were served by the same woman who had served them the other time they had come here.

"I know I should know that woman!" Helen frowned.

"Why don't we ask her name?" Sondra said. "Or if she knows you?"

"She doesn't," Helen shook her head. "There's not a spark of recognition in her eyes when she looks at me. No, forget it. Let's concentrate on this delicious food. Sondra, you ordered us a perfect celebration meal."

"I'm glad you like it," Sondra said. "And now I'd like to make a toast."

They listened to her, watching her closely. She lifted her glass. "To two of the nicest people I know and whom I love dearly. I *do* want you to be happy. I mean that!"

Helen's eyes misted with tears and Dave beamed.

"How could I have been so lucky?" Dave asked in a husky voice. "How did I get two such wonderful girls?"

The supper had been nice but it had left Sondra keyed up and restless. At least she had done one thing. She had started down the road of forgiveness toward her mother and she welcomed the trip with joy. Things were beginning to fall into place. At least some of them — but she would not think about Cleve or Carrie's grandson or what to do about the inheritance.

When she reached Wild Willow, she hurried inside, hugging her coat against the raw wind. The lake rippled cold and dark, slapping at the dock. The fire was still burning and she added a log and poked at the embers.

She must have fallen asleep on the couch, for she was awakened by someone pounding at the door, shouting her name.

"It's Tom Vogel and I must see you, Miss Tracy. It's urgent!"

Sondra fumbled with the lock and Tom came bursting inside. There was a wildly excited look about him. His hair was rumpled and his jacket had been buttoned crookedly.

"It's happened!" he said. "Miss Tracy, it's happened!"

"I don't know that you mean," Sondra said, shaking the sleep out of her eyes.

"I know who I am. It's happened! My memory's back!"

She stared at him. Then he grasped her hand and shook it up and down like an excited young boy.

"Meet Thomas Terry Winterhall Vogel! Vogel was my stepfather's name. Do you understand what I'm saying, Miss Tracy? Carrie was my grandmother. I'm Carrie's grandson!"

27

Sondra couldn't believe what she was hearing. It came echoing to her like sound through a long tunnel, like a faraway cry heard in a dream. Sondra backed away from Tom's excited eyes. Her head was swimming in earnest now. She felt almost faint, as if she were a child's tower of toy blocks tumbling down, down, down.

"Tom, what was your father's name?"

"Phillip. Mother's name was Tonya," he said. Then with a touch of sadness he added, "They're both gone now."

Sondra sank into a chair. She had wanted this to happen and now that it had — she looked up into Tom Vogel's happy face.

"It's all so fantastic! The reason I came here was to see Grandmother. Well, you must know that there were hard feelings about Dad. So Grandmother never really knew me because of that. I only saw her a few times. I visited her house once a long time ago, but I still remember it! What a grand old house it is!"

"You're going too fast for me, Tom," Sondra shook her head.

Tom laughed. "Oh, you don't know what a relief it is! I know who I am and why I'm here and —" he broke off, growing sober once again. "I'm sorry Grandmother died before I could see her. It was sudden, wasn't it?"

"Yes."

"I arrived just a day or two too late. I didn't have much money. It took all I had to get here. Fortune hasn't exactly blessed me. So I thought I'd see about a job at the new clubhouse. Then — well, there was that stupid accident — and you know the rest."

"Tom, where were you born?"

"That's an easy question now. Abroad. London. Dad died before I was born. Mother brought me back to America and eventually got married again to John Vogel. He adopted me. He's out West somewhere. After Mother died, he sort of drifted away and left me on my own —"

"Tom, you know I'm Carrie's only legal heir . . ."

Tom nodded. "Miss Tracy, I didn't come here to cause you any trouble. I didn't even know about you when I left New York to come here. I just wanted to see Grandmother. It had been so long and there had been so much unhappiness between her and my mother — it's a long story. I'm not even sure I know it all."

Sondra drew a long breath. At last she knew the mystery was solved. All she had to do now was act on it.

"Would you meet me in Quentin Hancock's office tomorrow," she asked. "Be there about ten. I'll phone him and if he's not going to be free, I'll let you know at the hotel."

"But why would you — well, okay, Miss Tracy. I'll be there. I tell you, I'm one happy man tonight! I know I'll never sleep a wink. I know who I am!"

Sondra closed the door behind Tom with a thoughtful

sigh. Carrie's grandson, the missing person she had been so determined to find, had been under her nose all this time!

She knew she could not sleep either. She thought of phoning her mother with the news and then changed her mind. She tried to reach Gretta but the answering service told her that she was still at the hospital. She was probably with Russ.

Sondra decided to go there. She had to tell someone.

When she reached the hospital, she went down the hall toward Russ's room. Gretta was there, bending over him. Russ was conscious.

"Gretta?" he said.

"Yes."

"Come closer."

"I'm close enough," Gretta said. "You shouldn't be talking so much."

"Have to," Russ said. "You know, being here like this, not knowing whether I'm going to make it or not, I've been doing a lot of thinking."

"You're too woozy with sedatives to think," Gretta told him.

"Not half as woozy as you imagine. I know you've been here for hours and hours."

"You're my patient."

"No, it's more than that," Russ said. "Isn't it?"

"Russ —"

"It's true. A man sometimes can't see the forest for the trees. I couldn't see you because I looked right over the top of your adorable little head. Gretta, I'm trying to tell you I love you. Do you hear me, I love you!"

"You're drugged. You don't know what you're saying. Let's just forget you said those words."

Russ's voice grew stronger. "Don't rile me, Gretta. *I love you!* You want me to shout it so everyone in this hospital will hear me?"

"No. Sh! Russ —"

"Come here. Oh, please, come here!"

Sondra could resist her curiosity no longer and slowly pushed open the door. She saw Gretta bending over Russ and in a flash, Russ had pulled her down so that their lips met. Sondra watched for a moment, delight singing in her heart. Then with a smile on her face, she closed the door and tiptoed away. She would not bother Gretta tonight.

There was one final phone call that night — from Helen Tracy.

"Darling, I heard what happened. About Tom Vogel."

"How on earth —"

"It seems Tom is spreading the word all over town."

"Well, you can't blame Tom for being excited, can you?"

"You must promise not to do anything rash!" Helen said anxiously.

"I won't. But I'm meeting Tom at Quentin Hancock's office at ten in the morning."

"But why —"

"You know why. I can't take what isn't mine. It belongs to Tom, not me."

"But, Sondra —"

"My mind's made up, Mother. I'm glad it's over."

"Sondra, listen to me!" Helen was nearly hysterical. "You don't know the entire story. I-I think it's time you did. I'd like to come and talk to you. Now."

28

Sondra went to poke up the fire. She put on a pot of coffee and sat on the couch before the fire, waiting. Helen Tracy arrived about half an hour later. Her face was ashen.

"I'm not going to marry Dave."

Sondra stared. "What did you say?"

"I can't marry him, Sondra. He's a good, fine, decent man, but I can't marry him!"

"Why on earth not? I thought you loved him!"

"I do," Helen nodded. "And he thinks I'm the most wonderful woman on earth."

"That's a pretty good basis for marriage, isn't it?"

"I told you it was time for you to know a few things. Personally, I thought it was time years ago. Your father didn't agree. Now, I don't see how I can avoid telling you."

"Tell me what?"

Helen paused and took a deep breath. "Your father wasn't my first husband, Sondra. When I was a young girl, your father loved me very much. At the time, I loved him too, but I was too silly and foolish to realize it. You

know how it is. We get smitten with moviestars or football heroes or the local rich boy. With me, it was Phillip Winterhall."

Sondra felt a rush of surprise leaping along her nerves.

"You cared about Phillip?"

"I thought I loved him. He was an exciting, rebellious, handsome boy who could charm blossoms off the trees. So secretly, in another state, I married him."

Sondra's mouth dropped open but she could find nothing to say.

"I went with him to London. I lived with him for one miserable month. I'm sorry to say that it didn't take more than a few days for me to realize that it takes more than starry eyes and rainbows to make a marriage work."

"I don't believe this!"

"It's true," Helen said. "To make a long story short, I divorced Phillip and he married Tonya almost immediately. In the meanwhile, there was Arnold. He came to London and brought me back to Lewiston. He married me. He got me out of a very nasty situation, and for that, I loved him dearly."

Sondra shook her head. It was all coming much too fast.

"But if you were married to Phillip, didn't Carrie know?"

"Only a few knew. Tonya, of course. And Arnold."

"But why didn't you ever tell Carrie?"

Helen gave her a wistful smile. "Oh, I wanted to! Many times. But Arnold never wanted her to know. It was a promise I made when I married him."

"Why would Dad ask you to do a thing like that?"

"He wanted to be the only man in my life. He wanted

no one to know that there had been someone else once —
he was funny that way."

"But why are you telling me all of this now?"

"After Phillip left me and married Tonya, they stayed
together for only a short time. Actually, I think Tonya
simply wanted to show me she could take Phillip away
from me. Tonya was like that. She married again later."

"To Tom's stepfather. Vogel?"

Helen gripped her hands together. "That's what I
came to tell you. Tom Vogel is more than likely his real
name. I only know that his name was not and never was
Winterhall!"

"But how do you —"

"After Phillip and Tonya parted, I saw Phillip again.
Just once. He came home to Lewiston. He phoned and
asked to meet me. I went, secretly, because if Arnold had
known, he would have been insanely jealous."

"But why when you left him, did you want to see him
again?"

Helen licked her lips and sighed. "Phillip was not a
strong man. He was ill. Things had gone badly for him.
Tonya had left him and borne the other man a son. But I
know for a fact that he and Tonya had no children of
their own. Tom Vogel *cannot* be Carrie's grandson!"

Sondra could barely grasp it all. "You mean Tom Vogel
is deliberately trying to cheat me? But how could he hope
to do that, Mother? He must have some kind of proof."

"Perhaps he'll have some falsified certificates or records — but I know he is not Phillip's child. So it will be
my word against his," her mother said. "Now, you must
promise me not to do anything foolish tomorrow
morning."

"Mother —"

"Yes, dear."

"Would you come with me tomorrow when I see Quentin?"

Helen nodded. "Yes, I'll meet you at his office. I'll tell him what I know."

Cleve Ridgeway had had an early dinner with Valerie and her father. Valerie had disappeared and Ed had gone to get his box of expensive cigars.

"There's a nip in the air tonight, but if you feel like a stroll, I'd like to stretch my legs," Ed said.

"Sure," Cleve nodded.

He knew the dinner had been planned with this in mind. Why else would Valerie have done the disappearing act? He also knew what was in store for him and he didn't like it.

They stepped through the glass doors and out onto the patio. The night hung heavy with autumn. Ed's elaborate backyard showed signs of preparation for winter. Rose bushes had been trimmed back, earth heaped around the roots and their branches tied and wrapped. Flower beds had been cleared and spaded. Piles of leaves had been raked and towed away.

They walked quietly under the ancient trees, leaves falling; Cleve held the cigar in his hand but smoked it very little.

"Cleve, the time's come. You've got your nose smack up against a big decision. I'm going to do a little arm twisting. I'm going to lay it on the line. If you don't take the job at the new clubhouse as manager, I'll have to get someone else. In fact, I've got a few that are after it right now. I can't hold off much longer."

Cleve turned the cigar in his hand and paused. "You want it straight, Ed?"

"That's the way I operate and you know it."

"I'm not interested," Cleve said. "I told you that from the beginning. I don't belong in any fancy clubhouse. I belong where I am, at Lewiston College."

Ed made an angry sound in his throat. "I thought you were a young man with a head on his shoulders! A little ambition in his pocket. Good sense on his side. Do you know what you're doing?"

Cleve nodded in the darkness. "I most certainly do."

Ed's cigar glowed in the dark and he swore under his breath.

"You're the most exasperating young man I ever knew!" Ed said. "Can't you think about Valerie for a change? All you're thinking about is yourself."

"It's my life, Ed."

"Valerie's got her heart set on having you out there at the clubhouse. It was her plan all along."

"Sorry," Cleve said.

"I'll stop all my contributions to the college!" Ed said peevishly.

Cleve straightened. "That's your affair, Ed. If you've been donating just to keep me in your favor, you've made a bad and miserable mistake."

Ed swore. Loud and long. Cleve tossed the cigar away. He watched it arch through the night, a miniature rocket, and when it hit the ground, he thrust his hands deep into his pockets.

"I can't be bought, Ed. I guess most of the people you deal with can. I'm a different breed."

"You're a damned fool, that's what you are!"

Cleve laughed. He felt the joy of the sound deep inside

him. It was as if he had just been released from a dark and dank prison.

"How dare you stand there and giggle like a hyena!" Ed shouted.

"I dare," Cleve said. "I thank you for the offer, Ed. I appreciate it, even if you don't think so. But you can write me off your list."

"And Valerie?" Ed asked in a glowering voice.

Cleve took a moment to answer. He supposed he had always known the truth about Valerie. But he had never seen it as clearly or plainly as he did right here in the pitch darkness of the autumn night.

"I'll handle that in my own way, Ed. I'd better go now and tell her that it's all off."

"Back so soon?" Valerie asked.

Cleve moved into the room and nodded. "I'm not much for expensive cigars, Valerie."

Valerie's green eyes flickered. "Daddy said he was going to talk to you."

"Yes. Just as you planned he would," Cleve said with a set jaw.

Valerie came to him and linked her arm through his. "Let's sit down and talk about it, shall we?"

He allowed her to lead him to a comfortable sofa and she put her head on his shoulder. Her dark hair brushed his cheek and he found himself going tense.

"I'm not taking the job, Valerie," Cleve said.

She drew back her head. "You're mad! You can't mean that. You can't spoil all my plans. You *can't* do this, Cleve!"

He looked into her lovely face and saw that it wasn't as perfect as he had always thought. There were harsh lines

around her mouth. They always appeared when she didn't get her own way. The mouth wasn't full and laughing like Sondra's, but rather small and selfish, and her green eyes had sharpened like steel points.

"I'm sorry, Valerie. But that's the way it is."

"I thought you cared for me! I thought you really and truly loved me —"

Cleve didn't know how to say it, but he knew he must.

"I'm sorry about that too, Val. It's just not going to work with us. It never had a ghost of a chance from the beginning."

Valerie stared at him. "What are you doing — kissing me off like some one-night party girl?"

Cleve swallowed hard. "That's a crude way of putting it. But, yes, I want to end it here and now."

Valerie stared at him and her face went white with rage.

"It's Sondra, isn't it? You're still in love with her! You thought I didn't see you slipping away with her the night of the reunion. But I did!"

"While you were being cozy with Lon Greene?"

"Lon's got more manners than you'll ever have. You're an egotistical, hard-headed, unreasonable —"

"Say it all, Valerie. Let it all hang out," Cleve said. "Because I'll not be around again to hear it. Say what you want, but say it!"

Cleve got to his feet. He had witnessed more than one of Valerie's temper tantrums but he had never seen her like this.

"Get out! I never want to see you again!" she screamed.

He saw her grab for a vase and he knew what was coming. He ducked and the vase splintered as it crashed against the wall. He hurried to the door, and all the time

she was shouting wildly, throwing anything she could get her hands on.

He escaped the house and got into his car. Gripping the wheel, he took a deep breath. Well, at least he had gone out in style! Somehow, the humor of it all struck him. For a little while he sat there laughing like a fool. Then he started the car and drove away.

He was glad it was behind him. It was over. But Valerie would not be unhappy long. She would set her sights on some other likely man and history would repeat itself. He knew he was far from the first man in her life and he was far from the last.

He found himself driving toward the far end of town. When he reached the house, he saw a light on. It wasn't late. More than likely his father was watching television or reading the evening paper, shoes off, feet up.

He knocked at the door. "Hey, Pop. It's me."

In a moment, the older man had opened the door. "Come on in, Cleve. Wasn't expecting you."

"I just had a fight with Valerie. It's all off between us."

Cleve's father reached for one of the many pipes that hung on a rack by his chair and filled it with tobacco.

"You don't seem surprised." Cleve said.

"I figured your good sense would rear up its head in the nick of time. Just as well, son. She wasn't the woman for you. She had her nose too high in the air. And no matter how hard you could try, you'd never equal her in that respect. You're down to earth, Cleve. Like me."

Cleve sat down in one of the comfortable chairs and stretched out his long legs.

"Ed wanted me to take over the new clubhouse. He's more than a little sore."

"Trouble with rich people, they think the chips are always going to fall their way. But defeat comes to all of us, Cleve, at one time or another."

"Ed will find someone else," Cleve said. "Plenty of men will jump at the chance. Was I wrong to say no?"

His father pointed the stem of his pipe at Cleve and jabbed it in the air for emphasis. "One thing I tried to teach you was to do what seems right for yourself. Even if it's just digging ditches. Do it. If it's working at the college, do it. If it's driving a truck, do it."

"The college is right for me," Cleve said firmly.

"Then you've just answered your own question."

Cleve laughed. "It seems every time I talk to you, Pop, that's what I end up doing."

"You're just using me for a sounding board."

Cleve nodded slowly. He thought back over his life, the past two years in particular, and he knew that he'd made more than his share of mistakes. He hadn't admitted the truth to himself. He had pretended to be what he wasn't, a cardinal sin in his father's book.

But the shackles were broken, the blinders were off and the lump of pride in his throat was due to be swallowed. Either that or go down a lonely road for the rest of his life living with mistakes and starving of loneliness on his male vanity.

Cleve got to his feet. He looked at his watch and decided it was too late to do anything about it tonight. But there was always tomorrow.

"Going so soon?"

Cleve nodded. "Got some sorting out to do, Pop. Do me a favor, would you?"

"Sure."

"Double up your fist and hit me right here! Hard!" he said, tapping his chin.

Cleve's father laughed and puffed at his pipe. "For not taking Ed DeReuss's offer?"

"No, for being a fool and a hardhead and a few other choice things, two years ago."

His father smiled and clamped a hand on Cleve's shoulder.

"Good luck, son. Let me know how it works out . . ."

29

"Good morning, ladies," Quentin Hancock said, as Sondra and her mother entered his office the next morning. "Sit down, please. Tell me what I can do to help you."

Sondra exchanged a look with her mother and told him what had happened. Quentin frowned.

"You mean Tom Vogel is claiming to be Carrie's grandson?" Quentin asked.

"He'll be here soon. I asked him to meet us here. Mother feels he's lying, that he can't possibly be who he claims."

The buzzer sounded on Quentin's desk and his secretary announced that Tom Vogel had arrived.

"Send him in," he said crisply.

Tom Vogel stepped into the room with a studious scowl on his face. He shook hands with Quentin and stared at Sondra's mother. Sondra introduced them and Helen gave him a curt nod.

"Well, Mr. Vogel, I understand that you claim to be Carrie Winterhall's grandson, son of Phillip Winterhall and Tonya Barrett Winterhall, is that correct?"

Tom licked his lips uneasily. "Yes, sir. I am. I'm sorry if

I've stirred up a hornet's nest, but the truth is the truth."

"Do you have proof of your birth?" Quentin asked.

Tom shook his head. "No, sir. Not really. You see, I was born in London. It was right after World War II. They were rebuilding. I was born in a hospital that had been half bombed and burned out. Records weren't kept as scrupulously as they should have been. When they moved to new quarters—well, the records were lost."

Quentin gave Sondra a quick, meaningful look. "I see," he said. Quentin picked up a pencil and began doodling on a pad of paper. "I'm afraid you'll have to do better than that, Mr. Vogel. You don't really expect to base a claim on such a flimsy story —"

Tom looked embarrassed and he cleared his throat. "Sir, my Aunt Gladys is out in the waiting room. My mother's sister. She can tell you —"

"Your aunt!" Sondra said with surprise.

"I know this is going to sound a little strange," Tom said. "But it's the truth. She knew I was coming here to Lewiston and she planned to follow in a few days. Well, she didn't hear from me — that was during the time when I had the accident and was in the hospital and couldn't remember anything — so she came on anyway, worried about me. Well, she found out what had happened when she got here. She even came to see me and told me that she knew me, but honest to God, she was like a stranger to me. I couldn't believe her."

"Then you knew all along who you were?" Quentin asked sharply.

"No. She didn't really tell me anything. She said she didn't want to confuse me, just told me where she was staying and where she was working, so that when I did remember, I could find her."

"Mr. Vogel —"

"She's outside. Let me bring her in."

Tom rushed away and reappeared with a wan-looking woman whom Sondra recognized immediately. It was the waitress who worked at the Chalet, the woman her mother thought seemed familiar.

"You're Tonya's sister?" Helen asked sharply.

The woman nodded. "Yes, I am. Gladys Shaw is my name."

"Yes," Helen said thoughtfully. "There is a faint resemblance."

"I understand Tom wants me to tell you about his birth," Gladys said. "It was in London. I was there."

"I say you're lying!" Helen said, getting to her feet. "This man is not Phillip's son."

Gladys Shaw gave Helen Tracy a hard glance. "You're mistaken. *I was there!* Tom was born to Phillip and Tonya. I have some friends in London who could substantiate this, if you want me to get in touch with them."

"I think you'd better," Quentin said firmly. "And might I remind you what the penalty is for attempted fraud in this state!"

Tom sat very still. He looked at the tips of his shoes. Sondra wrung her cold hands together, uncertain. They were getting nowhere fast. Just parrying back and forth, thrust and dodge, dodge and thrust, and she didn't know what to believe.

The phone rang on Quentin's desk.

"Excuse me," he said with a trace of annoyance, for he had left word with his secretary that he wasn't to be disturbed.

He listened for a moment and sat up straighter. "Thank

you, Miss Edgar. Yes, please bring the envelope over at once."

He hung up with a thoughtful look. He seemed pleased, and Sondra wondered what the call had been all about. Why was Diane coming here?

Quentin Hancock folded his hands on the desk. He gave them all a smile.

"Mr. Vogel, Mrs. Shaw, if you don't mind waiting a few minutes, I think we can clarify all of this very quickly."

Gladys Shaw nodded coolly. "Of course. The quicker the better. The Winterhall estate belongs rightfully to Tom. I intend to see that he fights for it."

"Carrie's will is iron tight. I drew it up myself."

"The court will decide," Gladys said. "I will see to it that Phillip Winterhall is exposed for the scoundrel that he was. Carrie will spin in her grave when I'm through telling all I know —"

"No," Sondra said, leaping to her feet. "No! I don't want that, Quentin. I want this settled — out of court —"

Gladys smiled, pleased. Tom gave Sondra a nervous look and tugged at his sleeves.

"I'll handle this, Sondra," Quentin said. "Please, let's all of us stay calm, shall we?"

The office grew still. There was only the creak of a chair to break the silence, the clearing of a throat, the steady tap of Tom's foot against the floor. Gladys Shaw sat like a queen bee, smiling to herself. Helen looked pale and upset. Sondra's heart was churning.

Then Diane Edgar stepped in, nodded to them all, and put the envelope on Quentin's desk. He opened it. The few sheets of paper made a hissing noise as they slid to the

top of the desk. Quentin read them quickly and he looked up, staring at Tom Vogel.

"I have a report here, Mr. Vogel. It gives your true name as Thomas Terry Vogel, nicknamed Sonny. You were born in Philadelphia. I have the name of the doctor who attended your mother. I have the complete statistics. Your father was John Vogel."

"That's a lie!" Gladys shouted. "A dirty lie!"

Quentin held up the piece of paper. "This is a report from a police computer. It took a little while to run down the fingerprint, but Diane has done it. It states, and this is an official record, that you were born in 1949, Tom, three years after Phillip Winterhall died."

Gladys had gone pasty white and gripped her purse. Tom looked Quentin in the eye.

"You don't expect to pull a cheap little trick like this and make it stick, do you?" Tom asked.

"Fingerprints do not lie," Quentin said. "It seems, Tom, you made the mistake of breaking into Carrie's house on Wyler Street one night. Sondra nearly surprised you there. You had to leave in a hurry, in such a hurry that you left a thumbprint on the brass doorhandle —"

Gladys bolted to her feet. Tom snapped at her. "Sit down, you fool!"

"Let's get out of here!" Gladys exclaimed.

"He's bluffing!" Tom said. "Can't you see that?"

Quentin shook his head. "I'm not bluffing. You might as well confess, Tom. You're Tom Vogel, not Tom Winterhall."

Tom looked at Quentin with a sneer on his face. Sondra had never seen anyone change so abruptly. He was no longer the likable, rather shy man who had

worked for her. This was a hard-eyed stranger with a look of hate about him.

"I'll get my own lawyer. I'll fight back!" Tom said.

Quentin laughed and Tom's face reddened. His fists doubled.

"If I were you, Mr. Vogel, I'd get out of town as fast as I could, before I advise Sondra to have you booked on breaking and entering," Quentin said.

Tom swore. He lunged at Quentin and then Gladys was dragging at his sleeve, calling him back, as she would an angry, mad dog.

"It's no use, Sonny. It never was any good. I guess I knew it down in my bones."

Sondra found her voice. "One thing, Tom. It was you who was in and out of Wild Willow, wasn't it? Just as it was you that broke into the house on Wyler Street."

"Sure, it was me! I had to get the lay of the land. I had to know what the places were like, some of the things that were in them —"

"Like the old table with the wobbly leg and the sachet in the drawer," Sondra said sadly. "Oh, Tom —"

"The amnesia was a fake too," Diane said. "It worked well into your plan. It made everyone feel sorry for you. You thought it would make your story stronger —"

"Sure!" Tom retorted. "I figured it would help. I didn't plan on any accident, but I saw a way to use it, so I did!"

"But you got tripped up by one little mistake, one little fingerprint," Diane said.

"And you were the big man with the big ideas!" Gladys ridiculed him. "I'm going. If you want to stay here and listen to all of this — you can. I'm going back to Philadelphia. I'm going on the first bus . . ."

"Wait a minute," Quentin said. "Sondra, do you want to press charges against these people? You'd be perfectly within your right —"

"No," Sondra said. "Let them go."

They went, hurriedly, cursing and yelling angrily at each other. When the door closed behind them, the office grew quiet for a moment. Quentin stretched out a hand to Diane Edgar.

"Good work, Miss Edgar. You've just saved the day."

"Yes," Helen said with a sigh of relief. "Those two must have gone to a lot of work and scheming to try a stunt like this. I'm sure Gladys had some people in London ready to swear that Tom was Phillip's son, maybe even a shady doctor who wanted a piece of the loose change."

"Gladys Shaw knew the story about her sister, Tonya, and her marriage to Phillip Winterhall. It's hard to say how and when they decided they would try to pass Tom off as Carrie's grandson. If the old woman had lived, it might even have worked," Diane said.

"I don't think so," Quentin spoke up with a smile. "Carrie was as sharp as a tack. Always was. No one would have fooled her like that."

"But I don't understand, Miss Edgar," Sondra said. "You were so certain Carrie *did* have a grandchild. Terry! Were you wrong?"

Diane Edgar glanced at Helen Tracy and then nodded quickly. "It would seem so. I listened to rumors. I forgot my own motto. I should have stuck to pure fact. I'm sorry."

Diane Edgar picked up her things, said good-bye, and quickly disappeared. Then Quentin smiled at them.

"So, Sondra, it seems there will be no further questions

as to your right to the estate, moral or otherwise," he said.

"I'll still feel strange taking it," she said.

They prepared to go. Sondra shook Quentin's hand and thanked him for everything. They walked out of the office, rode the elevator to the street level and walked into the autumn sunlight.

Helen's hand was shaking on Sondra's arm.

"Are you all right, Mother?" Sondra asked anxiously. "You look so pale."

"Could we have some coffee? In a quiet place. I-I must talk to you."

"But what now?" Sondra asked. "Everything's settled."

"Not quite."

They found a small café down the street. It was quiet, nearly empty. They took a cozy booth, and when the coffee came, Helen didn't even taste it. Her hands were still trembling.

"I don't want you to feel strange about taking Carrie's estate, Sondra."

"I can't help it. I do."

"No. You mustn't. It's yours. It's truly yours. I didn't tell you all of the story last night. I held back the most important part. At first, I intended to tell you all of it, then I thought I saw a way that I could keep my secret. I suppose I still could and no one would be the wiser."

"I don't understand —"

"It *is* time you knew. It's way past time, in fact. Remember when I told you Phillip Winterhall came back to Lewiston and asked to see me?"

"Yes."

"I think he knew that his time on this earth was short.

He wanted to see his mother, but me as well. To ask one very important question."

Helen paused and her eyes were shadowed, her voice very low.

"He came to ask about his child. *Our* child. His and mine. He came to ask about you, Sondra."

Sondra couldn't move. Helen's eyes brimmed with tears and they spilled over, trickling down her cheeks.

"What did you say, Mother?" Sondra gasped.

"You're Phillip's child, Sondra. When Arnold came to London to bring me home, he knew I was to have a child. But he was forgiving and kind. He wanted the child to be known as *his* child. I was never to tell, not ever — not anyone — that it was any different. I was alone, almost penniless, uncertain what to do. Arnold Tracy was a godsend —"

Sondra's ears were ringing.

"No. This can't be true!"

"I'm sorry, darling, it is. You've no idea how many times I've wanted to tell you the truth. But Arnold loved you so much and you adored him. Besides, I had promised."

Sondra's voice was hushed, awed. "I'm Carrie's granddaughter? *I* am the missing grandchild I've been looking for!"

"Yes, dear," her mother said. "Yes."

30

THE WORLD stopped spinning for Sondra. She was aware of the oddest things. A scar on the tabletop, a worn spot in the carpeting, the cool leather of the booth, the sight of her own hands clenching the coffee cup so tightly that it seemed she would crush it into a hundred pieces.

"I wish there had been some easier way to have told you, Sondra."

"And Carrie never knew?"

"Not until two years ago. I simply could not keep it any longer. It had weighed heavily on my conscience for these many years. Remember when Carrie had a spell with her heart about that time? I feared she might die not knowing the truth. So I told her."

"Two years ago? About the time that you and Dad —"

Helen lowered her head for a moment. "Yes."

Sondra understood everything then in a flash of light that shook her to the core.

"It was *me* that came between you and Dad!"

"I had broken my promise to him. We quarreled bitterly about it. But I trusted Carrie. She promised not to tell you. But then, she hardly had a chance, did she? You

left for Los Angeles, all broken up because Arnold and I had separated."

Sondra felt hollow inside, physically ill. "Oh, no, no," she said with despair, shaking her head.

"Don't blame yourself. If you must blame anyone, blame me for being weak, for making a bad mistake when I was young, or blame Arnold for his misguided pride — but never yourself."

"And Carrie knew who I was! If only I had known too . . ."

"It was almost as if you sensed you belonged to her, Sondra. As a little girl, you were drawn to her. Arnold wanted to stop your visits to Carrie. I couldn't. You loved her and she loved you. It seemed right that grandmother and granddaughter be together. Arnold finally relented, but I don't think he was ever really comfortable with that situation."

"But that means I'm not Sondra Tracy at all. I'm really Sondra Winterhall!"

Sondra stared out the window, needing to see the rest of the world, to be reminded that on the busy street life was going on as if nothing was happening here in this room.

At last she turned back to her mother. "This is why you were going to call it off with Dave! It makes sense now."

"In a way, it's a relief to have the secret out at last. I'm not sure Dave will understand. I've made such foolish mistakes."

"You were going to give up a man you love, a new life of happiness, just to protect me?"

In that moment, Sondra realized how much her mother loved her, had always loved her. She felt deep shame and regret for all the times she had been so cold and distant

toward her, when she had doubted her and wanted to escape from her.

"Oh, Mother, what can I say?" Sondra asked.

"I must tell Dave. I suppose the sooner the better."

"Let's do it now," Sondra said. "His office isn't far. Maybe I can help make it easier. Let me do this for you —"

"Thank you, Sondra. All right."

She phoned Dave at his office and asked him to join them. He came immediately and sat down in the booth beside them.

"What's up?" he asked. "What's happened?"

Helen Tracy couldn't seem to find words to explain. Sondra reached out and took Dave's hand.

"Uncle Dave —"

"What is it, pet?"

"If I told you that I wasn't really me, would you still love me?"

Dave laughed. "What kind of crazy talk is this?"

"I'm not Arnold Tracy's daughter. I'm Phillip Winterhall's."

Dave stared at her. It took a moment for the truth to strike home. Dave's gaze tore away from her and went to her mother.

"Helen —"

"It's a long story, Dave. But it's true."

Dave swallowed hard. "I knew you saw Phillip a few times but —"

"I married him," Helen said. "Like a moth drawn to the flame — I married him. Arnold knew the whole story. He took Sondra as his own, loved her, as his own —"

Dave reached out and took Helen's hands in his. "All I need to know now is, do you love me?"

Her eyes filled with tears. "More than you'll ever know."

Dave laughed. "Then what else matters? I'll answer that. Nothing. Absolutely nothing!"

Sondra left them a few minutes later, lost in each other. They scarcely knew when she had gone. Now it seemed everything was right in the world but herself. Who was she? Sondra Winterhall. But who was Sondra Winterhall? She didn't know.

Sondra drove aimlessly around Lewiston for nearly an hour. Then she found herself going to Gretta's office building and slipping inside. She knocked at Gretta's private office and called to her. "I have to talk to you."

"What's happened? You look so —"

"How's Russ?" Sondra interrupted.

"He's improving. We'll talk about him later. What's happened?"

"Everything. Gretta, who am I?"

Gretta laughed. "Silly. You're my best friend. My childhood chum. My slightly daffy friend."

"Do names matter?"

"Names?"

"If I were to tell you my name wasn't really Sondra Tracy, what would you say?"

"That I would see about getting you a room in the psychiatric ward. I think you'd better come in and sit down and tell me what's bothering you."

Somehow Sondra told her the entire story. The words came pouring out. She couldn't have stopped them if she'd tried. Gretta looked startled but didn't say a word, and when Sondra had finished at last, Gretta gave her a warm smile.

"You're just Sondra to me, old friend. You always will be."

"But I'm not sure who I am any more. Or what I should be or —"

"In all respects, Arnold Tracy was your father. He loved you so much he wanted you never to know that he wasn't your real father."

"I keep remembering all the sweet things he did for me."

"You did as much for him," Gretta said. "I used to envy the way it was between you and your father."

"I'm off balance, Gretta. I'm falling down through a deep, dark tunnel and there's no end in sight."

"But everything's come out right. You felt so guilty about accepting Carrie's estate —"

Sondra got to her feet.

"I'm keeping you. I know how busy you are. And I know how you must be worrying about Russ. He will be all right, won't he?"

"He's much better today," Gretta said. "I expect a full and speedy recovery and, Sondra —"

"I know what's happened and I'm so glad for you both," Sondra said. "You love each other. If only —"

Sondra suddenly turned. She hurried out of the building and back to her car. She didn't know where she was going. But the wheels turned under her, she threaded through traffic, and for a while she simply drove around the town, looking at landmarks, driving by the school she'd attended and all the old haunts. Memories were rich around her.

She visited her father's grave — Arnold Tracy's grave — and for a long time she stood there with head bowed. Then she drove to Carrie's house and went inside. She

would not have to leave it now. She could keep it. It was hers. Rightfully hers. By blood, by the love of a woman who had been her grandmother.

"We'll have tea," Grandmother used to say. "With cookies. Will you get the cups, Sondra?"

She went to the cupboard, reached in and brought out the fragile cup with the roses on the side and held it warmly in her hand. Oh, to turn back the days, the hours, the years! If only she could have once looked at Carrie Winterhall and called her Grandmother!

"But we had so much," Sondra thought. "So very much."

All those times together, those happy, happy times! Thank God her mother had let her come, that Arnold, too, had not stopped her from coming here. At least she had this much.

She had no idea she had stayed at the house so long until she looked out the window and saw that it was nearly dusk. She left the house and got in her car, but she couldn't bring herself to go back to Wild Willow just yet. Instead, she went down the street and stopped at the barricade.

She felt hollowed out, a tree ready to break in the first strong wind.

' "Sondra —"

It was Cleve. He stood with his collar turned against the wind, coat unbuttoned, his tie fluttering, his dark hair mussed.

"I've been looking everywhere for you, Sondra. Gretta was worried about you. I should have known I'd find you here."

"I've come home, Cleve," she said, foolish tears in her eyes. "But home is gone. Cleve — home is gone!"

"Gretta told me what happened."

"She told you?"

"She knew I'd want to know, that I'd understand how you feel now."

"I feel nothing," she said with despair. "Nothing I counted on has lasted. I'm not even Sondra Tracy anymore — not really."

Cleve moved toward her. "What's in a name? You're no different than you ever were."

Sondra looked at him. He reached out and touched her face and rubbed away her tears.

"This was home," she said, motioning to the spot where once the house had stood. "Now, it's gone. Vanished, like smoke on the air, and Carrie's house — that's not home either."

Cleve shook his head. "No, darling. Home isn't a house, a place, a room, a town. Home is where the heart is . . ."

"But where is my heart?"

Cleve's eyes were gentle and warm. "I had hoped with me," he said. "Darling, I love you. I'll always love you."

"Are you still playing some cruel little game?"

"When you went away to L.A. the first time after you'd quarreled with me and said you couldn't marry me, I went through all kinds of hell, Sondra. First, I was outraged and angry. If you'd come crawling on your knees to me then, I would have said no. But time tempers things. It makes us mellow."

She shook her head. "Cleve, let's not talk about it —"

"We *have* to talk about it. I told you I loved you, that I had always loved you and it's true. Oh, I tried to forget. I sought to redeem myself with Valerie. It never could have worked. Because it's you, Sondra. It's always been you —"

"Don't, Cleve, please don't say that — unless you mean it."

He reached out and took her face in his hands. He looked into her eyes so that she couldn't glance away. His gaze held hers. She saw the gray depth of his eyes and she remembered other times when he had looked at her like this.

"You love me. I know you love me, Sondra. I don't know why you can't say it. Tell me now. It's time."

She found she couldn't open her mouth. No words would come. He stared at her unhappily and then, after a moment, he shook his head slightly as if with despair. He turned and walked away, leaving her alone.

Like a woman in a dream, in some kind of bad nightmare, she watched him walk toward his car, shoulders hunched, hands in his pockets. She knew that he was going, never to come back again. Cleve could only come like this once. She knew him too well. But once was enough!

The fog lifted. The mist cleared. Miraculously the sunlight was laid at her feet and she saw clearly for the first time in a long, long while.

She ran with the wind around her, leaves stirring under her feet. Her voice rang out.

"Cleve! Wait. Cleve —"

He stopped and turned around. She ran to him and his arms opened for her. She clung to him and his kiss was as warm and passionate as she remembered. The old love was back, untarnished, unchanged, as strong and sweet and endurable as it had always been.

"Cleve, I love you. Don't ever let me leave you again."

"Never again."

"Will you come and live with me in Carrie's house?"

"I'll live anywhere with you that you want. Will you live anywhere with me?"

"Yes."

"Tell me why, Sondra."

She took his dear face in her hands and smoothed his wind-rumpled hair. Then, tenderly, she kissed his mouth and smiled at him.

"Because it's here in your arms. It doesn't matter who I am or what name I have or where I go. I know at last what I should have known all along. You're my heart, my love, my life. You're home."